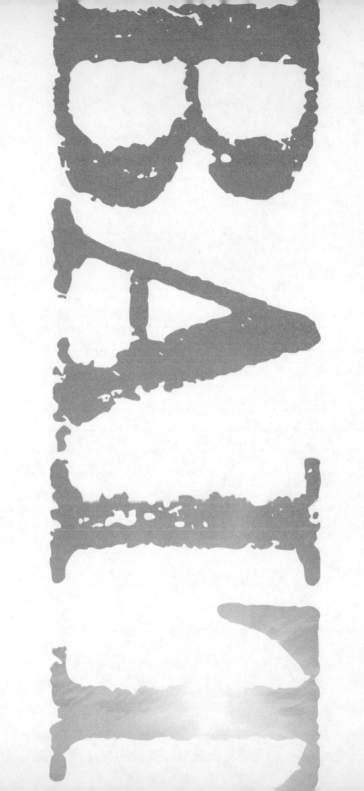

ALSO BY ALEX SANCHEZ

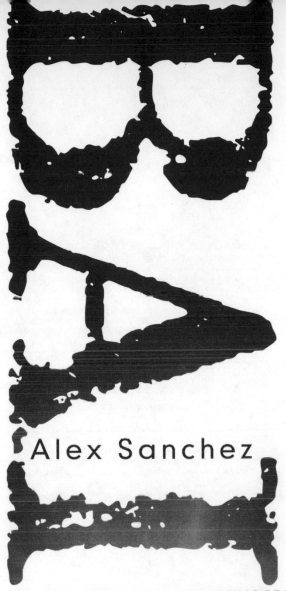

Alex Sanchez

SIMON & SCHUSTER BOOKS FOR YOUNG READERS

NEW YORK   LONDON   TORONTO   SYDNEY

SIMON & SCHUSTER BOOKS FOR YOUNG READERS
An imprint of Simon & Schuster Children's Publishing Division
1230 Avenue of the Americas, New York, New York 10020

Book design by Laurent Linn
The text for this book is set in Augustal.
Manufactured in the United States of America
2 4 6 8 10 9 7 5 3 1

Library of Congress Cataloging-in-Publication Data
Sanchez, Alex, 1957-
Bait / Alex Sanchez.—1st ed.
p.   cm.
Summary: Diego keeps getting into trouble because of his
explosive temper until he finally finds a probation officer who helps him
get to the root of his anger so that he can stop running from his past.
ISBN: 978-1-4169-3772-2 (hardcover)
[1. Emotional problems—Fiction. 2. Sexual abuse victims—Fiction.
3. Stepfathers—Fiction. 4. Mexican Americans—Fiction.] I. Title.
PZ7.S19475Bai 2009
[Fic]—dc22
2008038815

To the one in six boys and one in four girls

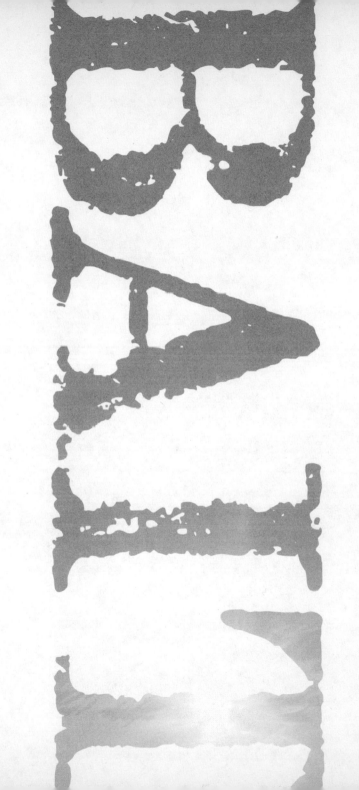

"If you bring forth what is within you, what you bring forth will save you. If you do not bring forth what is within you, what you do not bring forth will destroy you."

—The Gospel of Thomas, Verse 70

"THIS IS MR. VIDAS," explained Diego's court-appointed attorney as they headed into juvenile court. "He's the probation officer assigned to your case."

The stocky thirtysomething PO was shorter than six-foot-one Diego, but his grip was that of someone sure of himself, his voice calm and confident. "Good to meet you, Diego."

Diego shook hands warily. What would Vidas want from him? What if he decided he didn't like Diego? Would he recommend that the judge lock him up in juvie?

The courtroom looked like the set of some law drama—except for Diego this wasn't TV but real life. *His* life, spinning from bad to worse. He'd let himself down. Big-time.

He slid his lanky frame awkwardly into the defendant's chair, aware of the faint smell of his own nervous sweat. He wished he could change the channel and be at home, taking care of his aquarium fish or goofing around with his little brother, Eddie;

or at the beach with his best friend, Kenny, hunting for shells and riding waves; or at school, watching Ariel across the hall, hoping she might look over at him. He wished he could be anywhere else in the world but here.

As the bailiff announced the case, Diego's outgrown dress shoes chewed at his ankles. His crimson-colored tie felt like a noose around his neck. And from beside the brightly polished judge's bench, Vidas's hazel eyes peered directly at Diego—as if trying to see inside him, figure him out.

Diego glanced away, trying to act casual as he slid his hands beneath the defense table, where he tugged the cuffs of his long-sleeve shirt down to make sure they covered the cuts above his wrists.

Judge Ferrara, flanked by the American and Texas flags, gazed up from the file he was reading and peered over the front of the podium. "Your name's Diego MacMann? What is that? Mexican-Irish?"

Diego sat up, caught off guard. Wasn't the judge supposed to address the lawyers? Ms. Delgado, his attorney, nodded for him to respond. Little sweat blisters burst onto his forehead as he replied, "Um, yes sir, your honor."

At seven years old, he'd moved from Puerto Vallarta, on Mexico's Pacific coast, to Corpus Christi when his mom married his stepdad, James MacMann. In the process, "Mac" had adopted him. Nobody had asked Diego what *he* wanted.

"Well, that's interesting," the judge mused. The lenses of his horn-rimmed glasses made his eyes look huge and round as an owl's. "Sixteen years old . . ." He continued to read the file aloud. ". . . first time misdemeanor assault . . ."

The incident had happened at school, in the hallway outside the cafeteria on the way to lunch. Fabio Flores, a junior who painted his fingernails purple, wore eye makeup, and told the entire school he was gay, kept grinning at Diego.

It pissed Diego off. Why the hell did Fabio keep looking at him that way? Diego told him to stop, but Fabio kept it up until Diego couldn't stand it anymore. The anger moved like a pair of hands across his body.

He popped Fabio in the face—*only* one punch and not even that hard—expecting Fabio to block him. Or run away. Or *something*. He'd clearly seen Diego's punch coming. Why'd he just stand there?

His nose spurted like a fire hydrant, gushing blood all over the hall tiles. Girls screamed. The hallway monitors pinned Diego to the floor.

He knew he shouldn't have hit Fabio. He'd never wanted to hurt anybody. But even though he said he hadn't meant it, the vice principal suspended him for a week. And Fabio's dad had pressed charges.

"So does this mean," Judge Ferrara continued speaking directly to Diego, his voice turning angry, "that you've got an Irish temper or a Latin temper? Or both?"

"Um, I don't know." Diego stumbled over a response, as a bead of sweat trickled down his forehead. "Your honor, sir."

"Well, whichever it is"—Judge Ferrara jabbed his finger toward Diego—"you'd better learn to control that temper or I'll put you in jail. You understand that?"

"Um, yes," Diego replied, his voice trembling.

"Yes *what*?" the judge demanded.

"Yes, I understand, your honor, sir." Diego's heart pounded fearfully.

Judge Ferrara glared at him a long moment, then shifted his gaze to the prosecutor. "How do you wish to proceed with this case?"

While the prosecutor related the plea bargain, Diego only half-listened, rattled by his fears of being jailed.

Before court, Ms. Delgado had explained to his mom and him the plea deal:

"If you plead *not* guilty and a trial proves you *are* guilty, the prosecutor will demand jail time. But if you plead guilty and forego trial, the prosecution will usually support whatever sentence your PO recommends. Most likely you'll get probation. Maybe even less than that. It's your decision, but if I were you, I'd take the plea deal."

With his mom's agreement, Diego had said yes to the plea bargain. Anything to avoid jail.

Judge Ferrara now accepted the plea, ordered a presentencing investigation, and set a disposition date. Next thing Diego knew, he was back in the waiting room with his attorney, his mom, and Vidas.

"Now, you do whatever Mr. Vidas says," Ms. Delgado told Diego. "Okay? I'll see you on your sentencing date."

She said good-bye to everybody, and Diego's mom immediately turned to Vidas. "I want him to be on probation."

"Ma!" Diego protested. "I don't need probation. I'm fine!"

"If you're fine, why are we here?" She spoke to him as though he were a kid, despite the fact that he stood taller than her—even when she wore heels, like now. "I try to talk to him," she told Vidas, "but he won't listen to me. I don't know what to do with him anymore."

"You're the one who never listens," Diego muttered. He figured Vidas would take his mom's side like other adults normally did. But Vidas didn't. Apparently he was used to hearing such arguments.

"Hold on." He calmly raised his palms up between Diego and his mom, referee-like. "Let me explain what happens next. For the presentence investigation, I'll need to conduct a home visit, get your school records, interview the victim, and hear your side of the incident. Based on what I find out, I'll recommend a sentence to the judge. It might be probation or something else."

"But not juvie, right?" Diego's voice rose, tight and tense.

"Probably not," Vidas said. Once again he peered into Diego's eyes as if trying to glimpse things that Diego didn't want him—or anybody—to see.

"But it's too soon for me to rule anything out," Vidas continued. "A lot will depend on you."

Diego looked away. Why couldn't Vidas just assure him he wouldn't end up in jail?

"How is he behaving at home?" Vidas asked his mom.

"Most of the time he's a good boy. He takes care of his brother in the evenings and makes their dinner, he does his chores and homework. . . ."

Hearing her praise, Diego relaxed a little—until she added, "But sometimes his anger just explodes! I've told him he needs to control his emotions." She turned to Diego. "Why won't you listen to me?"

"Why don't you listen to *me*?" Diego shot back.

"And his father?" Vidas asked.

"His stepfather died," his mom said softly, "three years ago."

Diego glanced down at the floor, not wanting to think about Mac's suicide, wishing he could just forget Mac altogether.

"I'm very sorry to hear that," Vidas told his mom. Then he pulled an electronic planner from his herringbone jacket. "What's the best day for a home visit?"

"I have to work two jobs," his mom explained. "I only have Sundays off."

"Unfortunately," Vidas replied, "the visit needs to be during office hours, Monday through Friday, eight-thirty to five-thirty."

His mom glared at Diego and shook her head so angrily that the chrome clip fell out of her hair. "I can't keep taking time off because of your fights! You're going to make me lose my job!"

Feeling a little guilty, Diego stooped down and picked up the clip. He knew his mom was struggling to keep their family afloat. There hadn't been any life insurance settlement because Mac's death was a suicide. But even when Diego tried to help his mom with money from his Saturday job, she told him to save it for college.

As he handed her the clip her gaze softened. "Thursday,
I guess," she told Vidas. "Can you please make it later in the afternoon so I don't have to take the whole day off?"

"Sure. No problem. How about four o'clock?"

"Okay, thank you. I hope you can help Diego. Maybe he'll listen to you."

"Let's see what we can do," Vidas said optimistically. He shook her hand good-bye and turned to Diego, grasping his palm as though squaring some deal. Once again he looked him in the eyes, as if searching for something.

Diego tried to not look away, although he wished Vidas would stop doing that.

Outside the courthouse, Diego tore away the strangling necktie, a gift from Mac his mom had made him wear. Inside their old Toyota, he cast off the cramped dress shoes and changed into his well-worn sneakers, grumbling, "Why'd you have to tell him to put me on probation?"

His mom ignored the question and phoned the nursing home where she worked. Although she told them she was on her way, when she pulled out of the garage, she glanced at the clock and asked Diego, "Isn't it after your lunch period? We'd better stop to eat."

"I thought you had to get to work."

"Yes, but you have to eat." His mom *always* made sure he ate.

They stopped at a fish-and-chips place across from the seawall overlooking the bay. Inside the restaurant, he noticed that the Value Meal included a mini spyglass telescope. He decided to get one for his friend, Kenny, just for fun.

Sitting down at a booth, Diego's mom bit into a fried shrimp and commented, "Mr. Vidas seems like a very nice man."

"You don't even know him yet," Diego protested. She was always too trusting of people. "How do you know he's not some serial killer?"

"Ay, you're being silly." His mom pressed a napkin to her lips. "You need a man to talk to—a father figure."

"You don't know what I need," Diego fired back, recalling his previous so-called father figure, Mac. "You've got no idea."

Nobody but *he* knew the truth about Mac. His mom had never wanted to know, even when Diego tried to tell her. Now it was too late; it was over. Mac was dead.

Turning away from his mom, Diego lifted the tiny spyglass to his eye. He stared out the window toward the dark green waters of the bay, thinking—and wanting to forget.

AFTER LUNCH, Diego's mom jotted him an excuse note and dropped him off at school, telling him, "No more trouble, okay?"

He slammed the car door without answering. Couldn't she understand that he never *wanted* to cause trouble? He signed in at the attendance office and arrived at his locker just as the bell rang, flooding the hallway with students.

"'Sup?" Kenny smiled, walking up to him. "Glad they didn't lock you up."

He and Diego had been best friends since middle school—bonded by good grades and their shared love for the ocean.

"Nah, the PO has to do a report first." Diego bonked Kenny over the head with the mini spyglass, laughing.

"What's this?" Kenny grinned at the telescope and lifted it up to his glasses.

"Yo, MacMann!" Guerrero called from two lockers down. "So, who's your PO?"

Guerrero had already been sentenced to probation: for driving his foster dad's car without a license, crashing it into a telephone pole, and knocking out the power for an entire neighborhood. He talked and acted as if he were Diego's buddy, but to Diego he was mostly a pain in the ass.

"A guy named Vidas," Diego yelled back.

"He's a fag," declared Guerrero. To Guerrero, everybody was a fag.

Diego ignored the comment, his attention caught by a figure across the crowded hallway: Ariel Lamar.

To Diego, she was the most amazing girl at school, maybe even the entire planet. She was beyond cute: radiant, with skin that emanated warmth, and the world's most perfect breasts. Added to that, she liked tropical fish, the same as he did. He'd seen her at the mall's pet shop where he worked. But to his regret, he'd passed up two ideal opportunities to talk to her, freezing up each time.

"She's smiling at you," Kenny whispered to Diego.

"Nah, she isn't," Diego murmured, even though it looked like she was. He felt himself turn red as he smiled back.

"She's smiling cause she thinks you're dorky." Guerrero snickered. But at that moment, even Guerrero's annoying comments failed to faze Diego.

"Why don't you go and say hi to her?" Kenny suggested.

As if it were that easy. The mere prospect made Diego break out in a sweat.

"Go reel her in," Guerrero taunted, "and bring her back." Placing both paws on Diego's shoulders, he launched Diego

across the hallway. And as though pulled by the tendrils of
Ariel's long, full lashes, Diego felt himself floating toward her.

Her smile beckoned as though it were a lighthouse. Her green eyes sparkled like sunlight on the ocean. But as Diego almost reached her, a guy wearing khakis and loafers sailed in front of him, cutting him off.

"Hey, Ariel," Preppie Dude greeted her. And even though Ariel peered over the guy's shoulder, Diego whirled around and raced back to his locker in record-breaking time.

"Smooth!" Guerrero grabbed Diego's arm and play-punched him. "Real smooth!"

Diego shook him off. He didn't like guys touching him, especially some jerk like Guerrero.

"What happened?" Kenny asked.

Diego didn't want to admit he'd wimped out. "I think she's got a boyfriend." It was probably true. How could any girl that spectacular *not* already have a boyfriend?

"Well"—Guerrero smirked—"you can always go back to Fabio."

"Shut up!" Diego barked, wanting to pound Guerrero, nearly forgetting he'd been in court for assault only hours earlier. Luckily, Kenny pulled him back.

During the remainder of the school day, Diego tried to concentrate on his classwork and stop thinking about how he'd once again botched up with Ariel. It embarrassed him that at sixteen, he'd never even kissed a girl—although not for lack of interest. He liked girls. A lot. A whole lot.

In his room alone or while taking a long shower, he'd

fantasize about holding a girl in his arms, stroking her hair, kissing her lips. . . . He'd run his hands tenderly across her breasts and when she wanted more, he'd gladly give it to her. And afterward, she'd lay her head on his chest, happy and satisfied.

But in real life, if a girl so much as said hi, he choked up. It was hopeless. He felt like a loser.

When he got home that afternoon, he peeled his backpack off and sat at his aquarium, his thoughts swirling about Ariel. Had she really been smiling at him? Could any girl that amazing ever actually be interested in somebody with problems like his?

He gave his clownfish, Nemo and Gill, a tiny snack of dried krill and then played peekaboo with them through the tank glass. The saltwater fish required more care and attention than freshwater ones, but it was worth it for the hours he spent looking at their brilliant colors, imagining them on a faraway reef. He loved his fish.

A short time later, his eight-year-old brother's school bus stopped out front. He joined Diego, watching the clown fish dart in and out of the rose-colored anemone. While Eddie jabbered about his school day, Diego mostly just listened and let him talk. He didn't mention his appearance in court. His mom had told him not to, since his little brother looked up to him so much.

After sitting for a while leaning into each other, the boys started horsing around. Diego had been teaching Eddie to box so he could defend himself if anybody tried to mess with him.

"Keep your fists up." Diego taught him like he'd learned from boxers on TV.

Eddie loved the horseplay, giggling as his older brother fought off his punches but ultimately let him triumph.

Since their mom didn't get home from her night job till after nine, it fell upon Diego to make dinner and help Eddie with homework. Eddie sat at the kitchen table with his schoolbooks, asking Diego questions while Diego boiled noodles, fried ground beef, and heated tomato sauce. Mac had taught him to cook—mostly basic stuff like spaghetti and burgers.

Tonight, after they'd cleaned up the kitchen and put the plates in the dishwasher, Eddie watched TV and Diego went to his room to do his own homework. But the loser feelings about his botch-up with Ariel kept gnawing at him. Leaving his schoolwork aside, he walked to his dresser mirror and examined his reflection.

His hair was thick and black. And his eyes were nearly as dark, just like his mom's. His cheekbones were high, his jaw square.

"You're a handsome boy," Mac had often told him. Diego had wanted to be handsome, but not for Mac. Even now he could almost feel Mac's hand running through his hair, tousling it.

Diego reached inside his shirt and pulled out the elastic cord that hung around his neck. Fastened to it with two bits of wire was one of the first presents Mac had given him: a great white shark's tooth.

At the time, the huge tooth had barely fit into Diego's five-year-old palm. The triangle measured over two inches wide at the base and was equally long, its jagged edges tapering to a perfect point. Everyone in his neighborhood had wanted to see it, especially the boys. Filled with awe, they ran their fingers across the bone-smooth surface and gingerly tapped the tooth's razor-fine tip.

The tooth gave Diego a feeling of power and strength. Since the day he first got it, he always kept it on—showering with it, eating with it, sleeping with it. Sometimes he woke at night and carefully ran his hands across it, to make sure the tooth was still there.

One afternoon shortly after Mac's suicide, Diego had come home from school with his mind a whirlpool of swirling thoughts and feelings—similar to today. Trying to calm himself, he'd taken hold of the shark's tooth, as an impulse came over him. He lifted the underside of his forearm, where his skin was lighter-colored, and pressed the tooth's point against it.

There was no pain at first. His skin sank beneath the tooth's pressure. Then he pressed harder. The tip punctured the flesh and a heat spike shot up Diego's arm. With total clarity, he watched a bright red bead bubble to the skin's surface.

Slowly, he sliced the tooth's serrated edge across his flesh like a steak knife. It was only a slight cut, but deep enough for pain to flood his body—a sharp pang that diminished all his other feelings.

A tiny rivulet of blood oozed up from the cut and glistened on his skin like sparkling lights. The entire room suddenly appeared brighter, its colors more clear, every sound more crisp. He ran his fingers across the tingling gash and felt a little proud. He hadn't shed a single tear.

A week after that first time, he'd cut himself again. And the next week and the next. The whole area between his wrist and left elbow became crisscrossed with scars. Perpendicular slices. Bisecting angles.

Sometimes the pain was excruciating. He knew he shouldn't be doing it, but he couldn't stop. He didn't want to. With each cut he felt a new thrill—a release of some pressure that had built up inside him. He was letting it out.

To staunch the blood, he nabbed Band-Aids, or cotton balls, or gauze pads from the medicine chest. As those supplies ran out, he used toilet paper and Scotch tape, or anything else he could find. When he peeled the bandages off, they sometimes stuck and burned like fire.

He took care not to cut so deep that he'd need stitches, and if a wound began to look infected, he slathered it with antibiotic cream. He didn't want his mom to find out. The secrecy of the cutting brought back a familiar feeling from when Mac had been alive: once again, Diego had begun to live a double life.

His mom never questioned why he used so many Band-Aids. Perhaps she was too busy working to notice. Or maybe she just didn't want to know.

At school, a couple of teachers had spotted the cuts and asked, "What happened?" Diego's heart raced as he told them the same thing he'd told Eddie: "Just an accident."

"Do you want to talk about it?" one teacher persisted, obviously not believing him.

"No," Diego answered. Confessing how crazy he was acting would mean admitting it to himself, too.

"You shouldn't do that to yourself," Kenny had said, wincing at the scars. "Doesn't it hurt?"

"Yeah." Diego nodded evasively. "But I like it."

"I thought only girls cut," Guerrero had sneered when he noticed the marks.

To avoid attracting any more flak, Diego began to wear only long-sleeve tops—cotton tees mostly, the sleeves of which were pliable enough to pull down below his wrists. When his left arm got full, he started on his right: the excitement of fresh skin. And when his arms filled up, he ventured across his chest. With each cut he felt stronger and more powerful than ever. Like tonight.

He sliced the tooth across his skin, and for a moment all his confused and painful worries about Ariel, Vidas, his past, and the future disappeared. Somehow, he'd get through it.

IT MADE DIEGO NERVOUS how his mom went overboard getting their house ready for Vidas's visit. She scrubbed the kitchen till it reeked of pine oil cleaner; ordered Eddie to gather up his scattered toys and game cartridges; arranged little clamshell soaps in the hall bathroom, warning the boys, "Don't use these. They're for company;" and made Diego vacuum every room.

"Why do you have to make this such a big deal?" he protested.

"Because he's a guest. We need to make a good impression."

"He's not a guest, he's my PO!"

His mom had always been about appearances. Never mind the truth; what mattered was how things looked. And yet, despite Diego's gripes, it felt good to have the house so neat and tidy—the best it had looked since Mac's death.

Diego helped Eddie clean up his bedroom. Then he organized his own—plucking books off the floor, tossing clothes into the closet, and shoving junk beneath the bed. After he straightened his desk, he surveyed the room feeling proud . . . until he looked up at the walls. He'd forgotten about the holes.

Each of the half-dozen fist-size punctures marked an occasion when something had ticked Diego off so much that he had taken it out on the plasterboard. Once, his fist had struck a two-by-four wall stud, searing his arm with pain and spraining his wrist. That should've taught him his lesson, but it didn't. The next time the rage took hold of him, he punched a new hole.

His mom had made him cover up the punctures with posters. But he'd never dealt with the last two incidents. What would Vidas say if he saw the holes?

Diego shifted the bikini-clad supermodel poster to cover up one puncture, but it exposed another. So then he moved his death-metal poster, but that revealed another hole. He covered that one up with a sign that he'd gotten in anger management class: STOP AND THINK. That helped, sort of. The cracks in the plaster still showed, but hopefully not enough to notice.

On the afternoon of Vidas's visit, Diego arrived home to the smell of fresh-brewed coffee. His mom stood in front of her bedroom mirror, hurriedly brushing her hair and wearing a shimmery aqua-colored dress she usually put on only for special occasions like a Christmas party or Easter Sunday. Plus, she had on high heels. She *never* wore high heels at home.

Was she interested in Vidas? Even though she still looked pretty at thirty-four, she hadn't dated anyone since Mac. The mere idea of her dating his PO creeped Diego out.

"You don't need to get so dressed up," he told her.

"I want to look good," she replied, spraying perfume onto her wrists. She rubbed them across her throat and gazed in the mirror at him. "You need to change your shirt."

"Why?" He glanced down and noticed a stain from lunch. "You think he's going to put me in jail for spilling mustard?"

"Hurry up!" His mom gestured impatiently as the doorbell rang. "Go change!"

"No," Diego told her. "I'm not changing."

"You are so stubborn." She flashed her heavily made-up eyes at him as she brushed past.

He heard the front door open, followed by his mom's cheery voice: "*Hola.* How are you? Please come in. . . . Diego is changing clothes. He'll be right out."

She's the one who's stubborn, Diego thought, and hustled to his room. He threw his backpack onto the bed, changed into a new shirt, and checked himself in the dresser mirror, pulling the long sleeves down over his wrists. How could she harp on some miniscule mustard stain but not say anything about his cuts? Had she really not noticed them or was she just afraid to deal with them?

When he got to the living room, his mom was motioning Vidas to the big armchair where Mac used to sit. Upon seeing Diego's fresh shirt, she smiled approvingly.

"Hi, Diego." Vidas extended his hand. "How are you feeling?"

The question seemed a little odd seeing as how Diego hadn't been sick. "Um, fine," he replied and shook hands.

"Would you like some coffee?" his mom asked Vidas.

"Sure, thanks." Vidas sat down and rested a file with Diego's name onto his lap.

While his mom walked to the kitchen, Diego took a seat on the sofa.

"How're your classes going?" Vidas asked.

"Fine," Diego said, sliding his cuffs down. "No problem."

"That's good. What's your favorite subject?"

"Biology, I guess." As he answered, a school bus rumbled to a stop out front.

"I'm home!" Eddie shouted moments later, bursting through the front door. He stopped short at the sight of Vidas. He'd obviously forgotten a visitor was coming.

"Hi." Vidas extended his hand matter-of-factly, as though he'd encountered little brothers and sisters before. "I'm Mr. Vidas." He shook Eddie's hand. "What's your name?"

Instead of replying, Eddie glanced at Diego uncertainly, climbing onto the sofa beside him.

"Go ahead," Diego said, nudging his brother. "Answer him."

"My name's Eddie." He gave Vidas a shy smile.

Their mom carried in coffee and cookies, greeting Eddie and setting the tray on the low table in front of Vidas and the boys. Eddie took a cookie but Diego resisted. His stomach was in too much of a knot.

"For my report," Vidas explained while pouring cream into

his coffee, "I'll need to ask some questions. To start, how long have you lived in this house?"

His mom turned to Diego. "Four years?"

"No, six," he corrected. His memory was always better than hers.

Vidas clicked his pen and wrote in the file, following up with several questions about the mortgage and utilities. Then he asked, "Could you please show me around the house?"

Diego's mom led him from room to room and the boys followed behind, first through the dining room to the kitchen. Vidas glanced out the window at the backyard swing set that Mac had bought for Eddie. It barely got used anymore.

"Through that door is the garage and laundry room." Diego's mom pointed to the door but didn't open it. She'd avoided going into the garage since Mac's death. Laundry had become Diego's chore, although sometimes Eddie helped.

They proceeded past the hall bathroom with the unused clamshell soaps to Eddie's room, where they paused only briefly.

"And this is Diego's room," his mom said, picking up and quickly folding the soiled shirt he'd tossed onto the bed.

Vidas wandered slowly around the room, peering at the aquarium fish and then stopping to admire Diego's prized Eastern Murex seashell. It was almost impossible to find one in such perfect condition, with all its spikes and wings intact.

Continuing around the room, Vidas read the titles of some books and DVDs. Then he spotted the cracks in the wall beneath the STOP AND THINK sign.

Diego held his breath as Vidas lifted the sign and stared at the punched hole.

"Did you do that?"

Diego nodded, his face warming.

"Stop and think," Vidas said, tapping his head.

"I know," Diego mumbled as his mom shot him a sharp look.

Continuing over to the nightstand, Vidas picked up a framed photo of Diego with his mom and Eddie at Six Flags theme park. Diego had torn out the figure that stood beside them, leaving only a disembodied man's arm across Diego's shoulder.

"Who was that?" Vidas asked, pointing to the space left by the ripped-out image.

Diego averted his eyes, wishing he'd stored the photo in a drawer, and waited for his mom to answer.

"That was Mac," she said at last, her voice tinged with strain. "Diego's stepfather, Eddie's dad." She gently squeezed Eddie's shoulder. "Why don't you go get another cookie and play in your room, so your brother and I can talk with Mr. Vidas?"

Diego wished he could leave too. Their mom waited till Eddie was gone before informing Vidas in a quiet voice: "Three years ago, he committed suicide."

"I didn't realize," Vidas said, setting the photo down. "I'm sorry."

"I told Eddie it was an accident," she explained, grabbing a tissue from the dresser to wipe her cheeks. "Shall we go sit down?"

She led Vidas to the living room and Diego followed behind, feeling more and more agitated. It bothered him to hide the truth from Eddie, and it made him uneasy to see his mom upset.

Vidas once again sat in Mac's armchair and wrote in the file. Diego's mom dabbed at her eyes and cleared her throat, while Diego took a cookie, even though he wasn't hungry.

He hoped Vidas would shy away from asking any more about the suicide, like most people, yet Vidas kept going.

"I suspect the suicide is hard for you to talk about, but could you please tell me how it happened?"

Diego kept silent, letting his mom respond. She took a breath as if to strengthen herself. "He had a gun. I didn't like him to have it, but that's part of who he was."

As she spoke, Diego recalled the first time he'd seen the .45, in Mexico during a boat trip, and how the gun had seemed so terrifyingly loud, so powerful.

"He'd been in the army, in combat." His mom pointed across the room to the bronze star framed on the wall. "He liked to go shooting at a range. It scared me to have the gun in the house with the boys, so I made him keep it locked in the garage."

In his mind, Diego pictured the metal cabinet next to the fishing tackle. The gun had felt so cold and heavy when he pulled it from the cabinet and held it in his hands.

"I was at work when the police called," his mom explained, balling up the tissue between her fingers. "They said a neighbor had heard a shot come from the garage."

Diego slowly chewed his cookie, replaying his own memory of that day: how he'd come home to find the house crowded with police; his mom sobbing as she told him the news; and the sense of relief that seeped into him.

"They found Mac dead," his mom continued. "I was in shock."

Diego had wanted to see the body, but the police said it was too ravaged. Several days later, the remains were cremated and the ashes scattered off the beach into the Gulf of Mexico. Only after that did the reality sink in: Mac was gone. Then came the guilt, like a crashing wave. Diego knew why Mac had killed himself. It was because of him. Diego had wanted Mac to die, and Mac knew it.

"How did you meet your husband?" Vidas asked, interrupting Diego's thoughts.

"In Puerto Vallarta, where we're from," his mom replied. "He came for a fishing vacation and ate at the restaurant where I waitressed. He made me laugh right away. He was always a little crazy. I think that's part of what attracted me. We fell in love very fast."

Each time she told that story, Diego wondered: Had she truly been in love with Mac? Had he really been in love with her?

Vidas wrote something in his file and asked, "How did he and Diego get along?"

"Like best friends," his mom replied. "Mac was the dad Diego never had."

Diego bit into his cookie, recalling times when Mac had

in fact seemed like the greatest dad a family could have. The
fun, nice, normal-seeming Mac had brought white roses to his
mom, taught Diego English, whomped up Sunday flapjacks
with ice cream for everybody. . . .

But there was another side to Mac: the crazy, scary man
who drank whiskey till it spilled from his glass, got into yelling
fights with his mom over stupid-ass stuff, and came to Diego at
night like some hurt little boy. . . .

Vidas glanced up from his folder at Diego. "How did that
photo on your nightstand get torn?"

Diego glanced at his mom, hoping she would answer
again, but she gave him a cross look. "Tell him."

"Um . . . I ripped it." Diego's leg began to jiggle nervously
as he remembered the day after Mac's death, when he ram-
paged through the house, prying picture frames open.

"He tore Mac's face out of all our photos," his mom elabo-
rated. "I'm still mad about it. He destroyed them."

Diego had tossed the photo scraps into a metal kitchen
bowl, doused the pile with lighter fluid, and lit a match. The
smoke alarm went off with a piercing shriek, and even though
he pounded the noise off, his ears rang all evening.

Vidas tapped his pen on his folder and stared at Diego.
"What were you feeling?"

Diego recalled years of pent-up emotion that had exploded
with Mac's suicide, and in his hand the cookie accidentally snapped
into pieces.

"Um, sorry." He bent down to gather the crumbs off the
carpet and his mom spoke up, talking as if he wasn't there. "I

think what Mac did to him was a terrible thing."

Diego sat up, alert. Vidas gave his mom a puzzled look. "You mean . . . ?"

"Taking his life like that."

Vidas nodded and wrote in his folder. Then he asked, "What about Diego's birth father? Are you in contact with him?"

"No. I was only eighteen when we met. After Diego was born, he left us. I never heard from him again." She ran her hands across her lap, smoothing her satiny dress and asked, "Are you married, Mr. Vidas?"

Diego cringed. Was his mom coming onto his PO?

Vidas leaned back in his seat as if surprised by her question. "I have a partner."

What did that mean? That he had a girlfriend but wasn't married? He wore what looked like a wedding band, but it was on his right hand.

Diego deposited the cookie crumbs onto the tray. For the next hour Vidas asked question after question about his health, school, behavior at home, how he got along with his brother, his mom's two jobs and income. . . . Straightforward uncomplicated questions.

"Anything else," Vidas said at last, "that either of you think I should know?"

"I can't think of anything," Diego's mom replied.

As Vidas turned to him, a barrage of thoughts ricocheted around Diego's brain—about cutting himself, the shark nightmares that terrified him, the unwanted flashbacks that barged into his mind—of hands, their restless fingers moving about. . . .

But how could he mention any of that, when he hadn't even
talked about it with his mom?

"Nope," he told Vidas.

"All right." Vidas closed his folder. "I'll get your school
records. And I want to meet with you in my office." He pulled
out his planner. "Next Thursday. Four o'clock. Can you make
that?"

"Sure." Diego nodded anxiously. What more was Vidas
going to ask? When would he finally tell him whether or not
he'd have to go to jail?

"Good." Vidas jotted the appointment onto a name card
and handed it to Diego. "Be on time, okay?"

When they said good-bye at the front door, Vidas started
to pat Diego's shoulder, but Diego casually positioned himself
out of reach. He didn't like men to touch him—even if it was
only a clap on the back or an arm across the shoulder.

After seeing Vidas drive away, Diego retreated to his room.
Sitting at his aquarium, he watched his fish dart between the
tentacles of the anemone, and he thought about the visit.

Why had Vidas asked so many questions about Mac? Mac
didn't have anything to do with his court case. And why hadn't
Vidas scolded him about punching holes in the wall or tearing
up the family photos? Wasn't a PO supposed to chew him out
for stuff like that? He wished Vidas would just yell at him and
get it over with.

Later that evening, when his mom called Diego to set
the dinner table, an odd thing happened: Without realizing it, he started to set a place in Mac's old spot. When he

noticed what he was doing, it kind of freaked him out.

"What's the matter?" his mom asked at dinner.

"Nothing."

He didn't want to think any further about Mac, and he hoped Vidas wouldn't ask anymore.

CHAPTER 4

OVER THE WEEKEND, Diego tried to block from his mind any further thoughts about Vidas. On Saturday morning, he biked to the pet store where he cleaned out cages and tanks, shelved merchandise, and helped customers. He liked both the job and the money it gave him.

That evening when he got home, he boxed with Eddie for a while, teaching him to bob and weave by moving his head in a figure eight. Eddie giggled so much he almost couldn't breathe anymore.

On Sunday, Diego had planned to bike with Kenny to the beach, as usual. But it rained, so instead Kenny came over to hang out, play computer games, and trade seashells. They'd been swapping lightning whelks, sand dollars, and all sorts of other shells for years. Time and again, Kenny tried to bargain Diego out of his awesome Giant Murex, but Diego always laughed and told him, "No way! Forget it. Give up."

The following week at school was uneventful, except for a biology test about vertebrates and invertebrates that Diego aced. Mac—the *good* Mac—had always wanted to see Diego's exams and high-fived him when he did well. Now, Diego left his tests on the kitchen table for his mom, but only rarely did she comment on them.

When Thursday arrived, Diego decided to ride his bike to his four o'clock appointment rather than wait for the bus and then have to transfer to a second one. Besides, he liked to bike. He checked with the neighbors to make sure Eddie could go to their house after school, then he set off for the courthouse.

Unfortunately, the ride took longer than he expected. When he got to the court building, it was already 4:21. He punched the elevator button a dozen times before bounding up the stairs and racing across the waiting room.

A receptionist with graying hair was busy on the phone. Diego hovered over her, watching the minutes tick by on the big wall clock, until he couldn't wait any longer.

"Excuse me? I'm here to see Mr. Vidas."

Without interrupting her phone conversation, the woman glowered at Diego and gestured for him to take a seat. Diego narrowed his eyes at her, turned to the row of other boys waiting, and dropped himself into a chair. With each passing minute, his anxiety grew worse.

At last the receptionist finished her conversation. A moment later, she said into the phone, "Mr. Vidas? Your appointment is here."

While Diego watched Vidas walk out of an office and down the hall toward him, he braced himself to get yelled at.

"Hi, Diego. Come on back." As they walked down the tile hallway, Vidas gazed up at him. "What happened? Our appointment was for four o'clock."

"I know," Diego grumbled and explained that his ride took longer than expected. "Plus that lady back there kept yakking on the phone."

"Mrs. Ahern? Part of her job is to answer calls. Your job is to get here on time. Right?"

"Yeah," Diego muttered. Was that the end of the chewing out or just the start?

Vidas opened the office door and motioned him inside. "Have a seat."

Diego plopped into a green vinyl chair and glanced around. The cramped office was messier than he'd expected. A stack of folders and a jumble of framed photos cluttered the desk. The computer monitor was shingled with scribbled Post-It notes. Coffee spots stained the carpet, and a crumpled candy wrapper lay outside the wastebasket.

When Vidas sat down, the swivel chair squeaked beneath him. He grabbed a glass candy jar from his desk and extended it to Diego. "Want one?"

"No, thanks." Although he liked almost any kind of candy, right now he wasn't in the mood. He just wanted to get this over with and find out if he'd have to go to jail.

Vidas unwrapped a hard candy for himself, popped it into his mouth, and pitched the balled-up wrapper toward the trash can. It bounced off the rim and onto the carpet beside the previous one. Diego reached over, picked up both wrappers, and tossed them in.

"Thanks," Vidas said, sounding a little embarrassed, and opened the file with Diego's name. "I got your school records. You're a bright guy—mostly As and Bs. Your teachers say you're hardworking and resourceful. That's great. You should feel good about that."

Diego shrugged. He sensed a "but" was coming—and he was right.

"But you've also got some teacher comments indicating concern about your anger."

Diego slunk down in his chair, awaiting the inevitable lecture about his anger.

Instead, Vidas stared across the room at him. "You look like you've heard all this before."

"Yep," Diego said.

"What do you think your anger is about?" Vidas asked.

Diego hesitated. Nobody had ever asked him that. He wasn't exactly sure what Vidas meant. "I don't know. I guess I've got a temper—like the judge said."

Vidas glanced at the folder again. "I see you took an anger-management class. Was that helpful?"

"No, not really. Those things like breathing and counting backward? It's hard to remember that stuff when something happens."

Vidas rolled the candy around in his mouth. "You mean 'something' like the incident that got you charged with assault?"

"Yeah." Diego slid a little farther down in his seat.

Vidas picked a pen up from the jumble on his desk. "I spoke with the victim, Fabio, and got his side of it. Now I'd like to hear yours. What happened?"

Diego thought for a moment, deciding where to start. "I didn't like how he looked at me."

Vidas raised his eyebrows. "How did he look at you?"

Diego's heels started to bounce nervously on the carpet as he recalled the look—a casual smile that Diego knew all too well; a grin that masked something underneath. "You know. *That* way."

"No." Vidas shook his head. "I don't know. *What* way?"

"Like *gay!*" Diego sat up in his chair, annoyed. "People made fun of me for it. They'd be like, 'Fabio's smiling at you. He wants to be your butt boy.' Crap like that. So I told him, 'Stop looking at me like that!' But he just laughed and said, 'Like *what*?' He knew what he was doing. So the next time he did it, I walked over and popped him."

Vidas leaned back in his squeaky chair, took a breath, and studied Diego. "Did you consider talking to a teacher about it?"

"No. What was I supposed to say? They wouldn't do anything."

"Fabio is a lot smaller than you," Vidas continued. "How'd you feel hitting someone little like that?"

Diego shifted his feet, a bit uneasy. "I only meant to scare him, not hit him that hard. I figured—you know—he'd back away or run or something. But suddenly he was bleeding all over the place."

"That doesn't answer my question," Vidas pressed on. "Let's say you saw your little brother getting beat up. How would you feel about that?"

"Angry," Diego said guardedly.

"Why would you feel angry?"

"Because. He's my brother."

"And so you don't want to see him hurt," Vidas added. "That's called empathy. It's an important part of what makes us human. It shows you're capable of love."

So? Diego stared at Vidas. *What's that got to do with punching Fabio?*

"Why would it make you angry," Vidas continued, "to see Eddie get hurt but it's okay for you to hurt Fabio?"

"Because"—Diego folded his arms across his chest—"Fabio is a faggot."

Vidas turned silent a moment and crunched the candy that remained in his mouth. "What's that mean to you: 'faggot'?"

"*You* know! Queer. A guy who messes around with other guys."

Vidas took on that searching look as if trying to peer inside him. "Has anyone ever tried to mess around with you?"

"No." Why was Vidas asking that? "I'm not queer."

Vidas persisted: "Have *you* ever messed around with another guy?"

"No!" Diego repeated louder. Was Vidas trying to pick a fight? He leveled his gaze. "I told you I'm not a faggot."

To his relief, Vidas backed off. "Okay. Anything else you want to tell me about hitting Fabio?"

"Nope."

Vidas waited as if expecting more. "Are you sorry that you hit him?"

"Yeah," Diego mumbled, wanting to forget the whole episode. "But at least he stopped looking at me that way."

Vidas frowned as if disappointed and wrote in his folder.
Diego turned to look out the third-floor window. In the distance, he could glimpse the bay, and beyond it, the Texas State Aquarium. He wished he were there now, watching the fish, instead of here.

He returned his gaze to Vidas. "Are you going to put me in jail?"

"I think you're already in jail," Vidas said, and continued to write. "A jail you're making for yourself. If you want to get out, you're going to have to open up. Otherwise, nobody can help you."

Diego frowned. What the hell was Vidas talking about? Why couldn't he simply answer his question?

"I noticed in your school records," Vidas said, looking up from the file, "there's no mention of your stepdad's death. After his suicide, did anybody refer you to counseling or to the school psychologist?"

"No." With his thumbs, Diego tugged the cuffs of his shirt down over his hands.

"What do you feel about his suicide?" Vidas asked.

"I don't feel anything."

"You tore his face out of your family's photos," Vidas countered. "You must've felt something."

Diego remained silent. Why did Vidas keep wanting to talk about Mac?

"Pick three feelings," Vidas said, pointing to a wall poster of several dozen smiley faces, each transformed into a different expression labeled with a particular emotion.

Reluctantly, Diego moved his gaze across the faces and chose three feelings: "Angry . . . furious . . . and rageful."

"Wow," Vidas said. "That's a lot of feeling. It's good for you to verbalize it."

To Diego, it didn't feel good; it only made him angrier.

"When somebody commits suicide," Vidas continued, "we sometimes feel mad at them for leaving us. You think that might be part of your anger?"

Diego shoved his fists into his pockets. *Was* he angry that Mac had left him? The death had definitely made things hard on his family. His mom barely ever laughed anymore. Eddie had cried every day for months afterward. And during the rest of that school year, kids gave Diego weird looks, whispered behind his back, or acted like they were shooting a gun at their own heads. All of *that* made him angry.

"It's natural to feel mad," Vidas went on, "but beneath that anger is usually hurt."

Diego wasn't sure what to make of Vidas. Other adults had lectured him about his anger, but nobody had ever talked to him about hurt.

"The question for you," Vidas continued, "is will you keep taking your anger out on other people? Or will you deal with the hurt that's underneath?"

Diego shifted in his seat, uncertain what to answer. He didn't want to hurt other people. But what did it mean to deal with the hurt underneath? What was he supposed to do when somebody made him so angry?

"It's your choice," Vidas continued. "Either you deal with your anger, or it'll deal with you."

Diego pulled his hands from his pockets and sat up, expecting Vidas to explain what he meant.

Instead, Vidas asked, "Do you remember anything about your birth dad?"

The question took Diego by surprise; hardly anyone ever asked about his real dad.

"Not really," he replied, glad to switch the topic from Mac. ". . . Only this photo my mom had." He could recall the image clear as day. "My dad's standing beside her on a pier, wearing a sailor's cap. When I was little I used to stare at that picture for hours. Sometimes my grandma took me down to the ocean to look at the boats and I imagined one day he'd come back. . . ."

"How do you feel," Vidas asked, "about your dad leaving?"

"I don't know." Diego shook his head. He'd never put a name to the feeling.

"Come on," Vidas encouraged him, pointing to the smiley faces again. "Try."

Diego scanned across the poster faces, but none of them captured the hollow spot he felt inside, the empty place that was always there.

"It's like he never existed," Diego explained. "So why should I feel anything?"

"Because," Vidas responded, "he *did* exist, or you wouldn't be alive."

Diego recalled moments when he wished he wasn't alive, when he wished he'd never been born.

"You mentioned your grandma," Vidas continued. "Do you keep in touch with her?"

"Can't," Diego said softly. "She died when I was five."

"I'm sorry to hear that. What do you remember about her?"

"That she was the best cook in the world." Diego smiled, happily remembering. ". . . That her hands smelled like tortillas, and her hair like violet water. She had long silver hair. She used to sing to me—lullabies and stuff. She wasn't just my grandma; she was my best friend."

"You miss her," Vidas said.

"Yeah, sometimes."

Vidas lightly tapped his pen on the folder. "After your grandma died, who took care of you while your mom worked?"

"Huh?" Diego's mind was still on his grandma. "Um, neighbors mostly. Until Mac."

Immediately, Diego realized his mistake. He hadn't meant to bring Mac up again.

"What do you remember about first meeting him?" Vidas asked.

Diego rolled his eyes. "I don't know. I guess the first time Mom brought him home: He scooped me up into his arms, shouting, 'Diego!'"

It amazed him how vividly he could recall that—maybe because every other guy his mom had dated either ignored him or pushed him away like some pest.

"He would fly down for long weekends. While my mom worked, he took me to his hotel. We'd watch TV or wrestle on the floor. In the pool, he taught me how to swim. I wanted a dad so bad. You know, to talk to and teach me stuff. I thought he'd be it."

Vidas stared at him, waiting to hear more, but Diego dropped his gaze, not wanting to go any further.

"It sounds," Vidas responded at last, "as if some hugely important people have left you: your dad, your grandma, your stepdad. That's a lot of loss and hurt for a boy to carry around."

Diego glanced up, a tide of emotion tugging at him. Nobody in his life had ever talked to him this way. Suddenly the phone rang, startling him.

Vidas picked up the receiver, answering: "Probation."

While Vidas spoke on the phone, Diego tried to figure him out. Was he really interested in hearing all this stuff? Why? What did he care?

"Sorry to hear he's not feeling well," Vidas said into the phone. "Is he behaving? . . . That's good. I'll see him next week then. Thanks for calling."

He hung up and told Diego, "Sorry." He glanced at his watch and said, "We're about out of time. How are you feeling now?"

"Fine." It amazed him how much he'd told Vidas, and in a way, he kind of didn't want to leave. He wished Vidas could talk with him more. "When do you want me to come back?"

"Well . . ." Vidas flipped though his notes in Diego's file. "I think I pretty much have all the info I need for my recommendation to the judge."

Diego's legs began to jiggle again. "Will I have to go to juvie?"

"No," Vidas said. Finally, the straight answer.

"Thanks!" Diego exhaled a burst of relief.

"What I will recommend," Vidas clarified, "is that you be ordered to pay restitution for Fabio's ER bill." He glanced down at Diego's folder. "That's three hundred fifty-two dollars."

Diego's elation abruptly ceased. Nearly his entire savings would be wiped out. "Why do I have to pay that?"

"Because that's how the world works: You break something, you pay for it. Hopefully, this'll help you to stop and think next time you're tempted to punch someone."

Diego closed his fists and shoved them beneath his arms, angry at Fabio—and at himself.

"Second," Vidas continued, "I'll recommend an SIS—Suspended Imposition of Sentence. As long as you pay the restitution, stay out of trouble, and don't get into any more fights, your sentencing is suspended. You're a free man. When you turn eighteen, your record will be sealed."

Diego shook his head, a little confused. His attorney had never mentioned an SIS. "So will I be on probation?"

"No. An SIS is in place of probation. I don't think you need a PO looking over your shoulder. You already get good grades. Your mom says you behave at home. You help with your brother. You've got a weekend job. You don't need me keeping tabs on you. What you need is to find healthy ways to deal with your anger—through your studies, exercise, constructive things."

Diego still didn't understand. If he wouldn't be on probation, then how was he supposed to learn to deal with his anger?

"So, like, you don't want me to come talk with you anymore?"

Vidas shifted in his seat, looking a little uneasy. "It's not that I don't want to talk with you, Diego. It's just that my job is monitoring, not counseling. If you'd like to talk more with a therapist, I think that'd be great. I can recommend you to the county mental health center. You'd have to pay for it, but they have a sliding fee scale . . . although there's usually a waiting list."

Diego kicked the carpet with his heel, at odds with the emotions battling inside him. He didn't have money to pay some shrink and neither did his mom. Besides, he didn't want to talk to anybody else. Why had Vidas asked to hear about his life and listened like he cared, if he was only going to pawn him off onto some stranger?

"Can't I just keep talking to *you*?"

Vidas stared across the room at him. "Diego, my job is to evaluate your behavior and make a recommendation to the judge. I'm a probation officer, not a therapist."

"But you listen good," Diego answered. "What if you put me on probation?"

He said it without thinking. He knew he should feel ecstatic to be getting a pass on probation, but instead it felt like Vidas was ditching him.

"Look," Vidas said gently. "You see this stack of folders?" He laid his hand atop the pile on his desk. "I've got a whole caseload of boys and girls who need help really bad. Even though they're the same age as you, they can barely write a sentence. They've never held a job. Their parents are on drugs.

Some don't even have a home. You've got so much going for you, Diego. All you need is to open up and connect with people—other than through your fists. Do that and you'll be fine. Okay?"

Diego shook his head in frustration. Wasn't it obvious to Vidas that he'd tried to open up and connect with him?

The phone rang again and Vidas answered. "Okay, I'll be right out." He hung up and told Diego, "My next appointment is here."

Diego glared at him, not wanting to move.

"Come on," Vidas said, standing up, and the swivel chair squeaked beneath him. "I'll walk you out."

In the reception room, a couple of boys sat waiting for their appointments. One of them glanced toward Vidas, smiling eagerly, and Diego felt a weird pang—almost like jealousy. He wished *he* were that boy, so he could keep talking with Vidas, and have Vidas listen.

"I'll see you at your disposition hearing." Vidas reached out to pat Diego on the back. "Bike safely."

For a moment Diego let Vidas's hand rest on his shoulder. Then he pulled away angrily. When he got downstairs, he slammed out the door and got on his bike, pumping hard away from the courthouse.

CHAPTER 5

DIEGO RACED TOWARD HOME, feeling more out of sorts than ever. Why the hell had he asked Vidas to put him on probation? Was he nuts? He didn't need Vidas's help—or anybody's. Definitely not some shrink prying into his life and telling him how screwed-up he was.

He pedaled hard along the bay front, determined to sort his problems out on his own. To start, he wouldn't get into any more fights. No matter what. And he'd stop cutting himself, regardless of how much he wanted to. He'd be fine.

When he arrived home, he picked Eddie up from the neighbors. As they crossed the driveway, Eddie play-punched him on the shoulder, giggling.

"Not now," Diego told him. He wasn't in the mood to box. Not tonight.

He started to make dinner almost immediately: tuna casserole. Boiling the noodles and mixing the mushroom soup calmed his thoughts a notch.

After dinner, he helped Eddie with some math homework, further taking his mind off of Vidas. And later, in his room, he watched his fish swim around the aquarium, soothing him more.

The following day at school during lunch, he explained to Kenny about the SIS. "It means I don't have to be on probation."

"That's great!" Kenny raised his palm to congratulate him, but Diego frowned and kept eating his franks and beans.

Kenny let his hand drop, confused. "It's *not* great?"

"I guess it is," Diego mumbled. But it didn't feel great.

On Saturday, he biked to his job at The Pet Stop, eager to replenish his soon-to-be-wiped-out savings. The highlight of the day was a new shipment of butterfly fish. Even though he couldn't afford one, at least he could enjoy watching them at work.

The following afternoon, he biked to the beach with Kenny. It was one of those bright sunny days when it made him happy just to smell the salt air, feel the sun warm his face, and let the wind whoosh through his hair.

They chained their bikes to a lamppost, climbed across the dunes, and wandered down the beach, scouting for shells until they grew sweaty. Then they yanked their shirts off and raced each other into the cooling waves. For a long while, they body-surfed, tumbled, and splashed each other. Diego loved being in the ocean, feeling both its power and calm.

They'd ridden a particularly good wave into the shallows when a patrol jeep roared past across the sand, its roof lights flashing, heading down the shore.

Kenny squinted toward the crowd gathering around a life- guard stand. Two more jeeps were coming.

"Let's go look," Diego told him. "Come on!"

They sprinted out of the water, grabbed their shirts and Kenny's glasses, and ran to see what was going on. As they approached the throng of beachgoers, the jeeps' CB radios crackled. Some EMTs had climbed across the dunes from the parking lot and were loading an ashen old man onto a gurney.

"What happened?" Kenny asked a lifeguard with sunglasses who was writing on a clipboard.

"He got caught in a rip current."

"Is he dead?" Diego asked in a low voice.

The guard nodded grimly. "Rips are like a circle: They drag you out and under. If you stay on top and swim across, eventually the current circles back. But people panic and try to fight." He pressed his sunglasses up the bridge of his nose and looked out at the ocean. "The current always wins."

He returned to writing and the boys stared at the old man as the EMTs covered him up and carried his gurney over the dunes. It was the first time Diego had ever been in the presence of a dead body. It didn't feel creepy, like he thought it would. Mostly he just felt numb.

The two boys hung out by the lifeguard stand, each lost in his own thoughts, while the crowd dispersed and the jeeps drove away. Then, without saying anything, they wandered down the beach, until they had walked far beyond the last guard stand. There, the boys sat down on the sun-warmed sand, digging their toes beneath the grains, and stared out at the shimmering blue waters of the gulf.

"It looks so innocent," Kenny said.

"Yeah," Diego agreed. He thought how sometimes, especially when swimming, he'd get the sense that the shark from his nightmares was really out there, waiting for him.

The mist blew off the waves, lining the boys' skin with a thin shroud of salt. The setting sun stretched their shadows across the sand. And as ghost crabs emerged from their burrows for their night's scavenging, the boys returned up the beach toward home.

At school the following week, Diego ignored Guerrero's obnoxious attempts to be buddies. Instead, he focused on his classwork, remembering what Vidas had said about working out his anger through his studies.

And every time he went to his locker, he recalled Vidas telling him to find ways to connect with people other than through his fists. He peered across the hallway at the person he most wanted to connect with: Ariel.

She was forever on his mind. Each evening when he climbed into bed, he imagined her beside him. He ran his hands gently across her skin while she kissed him. Her lips felt tender as flower petals, her soft blond hair brushing his face, tickling his cheek.

One morning, between classes, he spotted her at her locker attempting to unload an armful of books. The stack, more than she could handle, began to totter and slip. Faster than a bullet, Diego sped toward her, arriving just in time to catch the books as they spilled from her arms.

"Wow, thanks!" She smiled and her whole face lit up. "That was sweet of you." One by one, she took the books from his hands and organized them into her locker, explaining, "I just came from the library."

He gazed at her, knowing it was his turn to say something. But his brain had frozen and not even the warmth of her smile was thawing it.

She finished putting her books away and asked, "You work at the pet store, right?"

"Um, yeah . . ." he replied, amazed that she remembered. In his excitement, words began to tumble out of his mouth in an avalanche. "Would you like to—you know—hang out with me sometime?" And equally abruptly, his boldness sent him reeling. "I mean I'm sure you wouldn't. You probably already have a boyfriend. And even if you don't, I doubt you'd want to hang out with somebody like me anyway."

With that, he spun around and stepped away. And just as quickly, he regretted his foolishness. Why hadn't he let her answer? Maybe she *didn't* have a boyfriend. Maybe she'd like to hang out.

He darted a glance over his shoulder and saw her staring at him, open-jawed, looking as if she'd just been sideswiped. Hurriedly, he turned away again, feeling more screwed-up than ever. Would he ever connect with a girl?

To make things worse, Guerrero had apparently witnessed the entire disaster.

"Yo, don't tell me you wimped out with her *again*." He stood at his locker, wearing a demonic grin. Diego tried to shove past him, but Guerrero rode his heels. "Look, if you're too gay to make a move—"

Diego whirled around. His hand sprang out, grabbing Guerrero by the collar, and slammed him against the metal lockers. "Shut up!"

Guerrero stood on tiptoes, his face turning red, as Kenny rushed over and grabbed Diego's arm.

"Stop it, Diego! Let him go."

The familiar sound of Kenny's voice snapped Diego to his senses. What the hell was he doing? He unclasped his hand from Guerrero's collar, releasing him.

"You're a wacko!" Guerrero sputtered, smacking his palms against Diego's chest and pushing him away.

Diego stumbled back, shaken by what he'd done. Hadn't he promised himself to stay out of fights?

"Can't you just ignore him?" Kenny asked as Guerrero strode away. "Why do you let him get to you?"

Without answering, Diego turned to look across the hall, hoping that Ariel hadn't seen the scuffle. He found her gazing straight at him, her eyes wide with concern. Worse still, a couple of her friends were also staring at him, shaking their heads and saying something to her.

"I didn't mean it," Diego assured her, even though she couldn't possibly hear him across the hall.

Nevertheless, she nodded as if she understood. At least he *hoped* she understood as she walked away with her friends.

All during afternoon classes, Diego pondered how easily he'd almost gotten into another fight. In his mind he saw

Judge Ferrara's thick finger wagging at him, ordering him to juvie. And he recalled what Vidas had told him: Either you deal with your anger, or it'll deal with you.

What if he couldn't deal with it? What if he wasn't able to stop fighting?

After school, when Eddie came home, he wanted to play and roughhouse as usual, but Diego pulled away, once again telling him, "Not today!"

Eddie lowered his head, sulking. "You never want to play anymore."

Diego stared silently back at him, unable to explain his fear: What if he lost it with Eddie? He didn't want to risk it.

That night he climbed into bed feeling more uncertain and afraid than ever. What if he couldn't sort his problems out by himself? What would become of him?

As he sank into a fitful sleep, his nightmares began almost immediately.

The recurring dreams were usually similar: He'd be treading water in the middle of the white-capped ocean. Alone. Stranded. With no idea how he'd gotten there. Waves crashed over him, buffeting his head, while a forceful current pulled at him. His weary legs sank heavily, like weights dragging down his body, as he searched for land or a boat. Something to hang on to. Anything.

Suddenly a tiny triangle appeared in the distance between wave peaks. A sailboat? Diego's arms sprang into the air, waving desperately as he shouted, "Hey! Over here! Hey!"

But as the triangle came closer, a chill rolled down his

spine. It wasn't a sail; it was a dorsal fin. A shark.

Diego watched, terrified, as the fin moved toward him. He wanted to scream, but his voice caught in his throat. Besides, who would hear him? He was alone. Powerless.

He took a breath, heart pounding, and plunged his head beneath the surface. Salt burned his eyes as he watched the gray form circle him. Ghostlike. Massive. Powerful. A tug of current radiated from each commanding movement of its tail. Only its silvery eyes remained fixed, keeping its prey in sight.

Diego thrashed the water with his hands, fighting the current, trying to back away. His heart beat furiously as the shark moved closer, its head swinging right, then left. Gallons of water pumped through its cavernous mouth. Rows of teeth spiked its jaws. With a flick of its enormous tail, the great shark charged.

But just as the beast rammed into him, the dream changed. A gunshot fired. Loud. Clear. Always a gunshot. And the weight of Mac's body fell upon Diego.

He woke up gasping, trying to escape. He kicked at the bedsheets, scrambling across the mattress, and slammed back against the wall as he shoved the body off of him. Breath pumping hard, he fumbled the lamp switch on, terrified of what he'd find. But there was no body, no shark.

His chest rose and fell, his skin glistening with sweat. The dream had seemed so real. He listened carefully for the sound of Mac's cigarette cough from his mom's room, the footsteps in the hall, the doorknob turning. . . .

But the house remained silent. Diego lay awake, waiting

for his fear to die down. As his breathing calmed, he peeled
off his drenched T-shirt, pushed aside the sheets, and climbed from bed to pull a dry shirt on. The dresser mirror tracked his motions as he stopped to stare at his reflection.

The crisscross of cuts and gashes carved into his skin made him look like a freak. A crazy freak. Slashing himself by day. Chased by a shark at night. Too messed-up to connect with a girl. Unable to stop fighting. Lashing out at people he didn't want to hurt. Trying to be normal—but failing.

Maybe he should just slice the shark's tooth deeper into his skin. There, just at the wrist. Watch the blood leak out and drip to the floor, growing into a puddle like the dark stain Mac had left behind on the garage's concrete floor—the spot Diego had tried to scrub away. Tried hard.

He slid back into bed and left the light on, thinking about what Vidas had said: He needed to open up, or nobody could help him. But he didn't want to talk to some headshrinker he didn't know. If only Vidas would put him on probation . . . The things that Vidas said made sense. Diego had felt connected to him. There had to be some way to convince him.

Just before Diego drifted back to sleep, an idea floated though his mind: If Vidas wasn't willing to recommend probation to the judge, then maybe his lawyer could ask for it.

The crazy idea was one of those half-dream thoughts that didn't exactly make sense. But when he woke up the next morning, the idea remained in his consciousness, giving him a weird sense of hope. And as his court date approached, a plan took shape in his mind.

CHAPTER 6

THE MORNING OF HIS COURT HEARING, Diego woke
up ahead of his alarm, filled with anxiety. He could barely eat
breakfast; his stomach was so tense. He put on his necktie without his mom telling him to and squeezed into his outgrown
dress shoes, determined to make a good impression.

During the drive to the courthouse he sat silently, rehears-
ing in his mind what he planned to tell his attorney.

"Do you feel okay?" his mom asked from across the car
seat. "You seem so quiet."

"Yeah, I'm fine," Diego muttered. He'd decided to keep his
plan to himself, having learned in the past how easily his mom
could be swayed by other people.

The court waiting room was packed with boys in baggy
jeans and unlaced sneakers, accompanied mostly by their
moms or grandmoms. On the far side, somebody's baby was
crying. After a while, Ms. Delgado arrived and headed directly

to the prosecutor. When she finished, she came over to Diego and his mom.

"Great news," she announced. "The prosecutor agrees with your PO's recommendation. Restitution and an SIS."

"Is that good?" his mom asked.

"Yes. Your son is very lucky."

Diego sat up in his seat, taking an anxious breath. "But, um, I want to be on probation."

Ms. Delgado furrowed her brow as though failing to understand. "No, *mijo*, you don't have to be. I thought Mr. Vidas explained that to you."

"Yeah, but—"

"There's the bailiff," she interrupted. "Our case is next."

"Why are you arguing?" his mom asked Diego.

"Case number six!" The tan-uniformed officer bellowed across the waiting room, causing the baby to wail louder.

"That's us." Ms. Delgado stood up. "Come on!"

"But I *want* to be on probation," Diego insisted.

She apparently didn't hear him as she followed the bailiff and prosecuting attorney.

Vidas was already in the courtroom from the previous case. He nodded hello, but Diego glanced away, not wanting to lose his resolve. Taking his seat at the defense table, he whispered to Ms. Delgado, "I said I want to be on probation!"

"*Shh!*" She patted his hand to shush him. "That's not for you to decide."

Diego slumped back in his seat, frustrated. Wasn't his lawyer supposed to do what he wanted?

"Let's see here." Judge Ferrara adjusted his horn-rimmed glasses and read from a folder: "'Diego MacMann pleaded guilty to misdemeanor assault. . . .'" The judge peered up and over the bench as if trying to recall Diego from among countless other cases. Then he glanced past Diego at his mom. "You're the boy's mother? How are you today, ma'am?"

The color bloomed in his mom's cheeks as she answered, "Fine, thank you, your honor. And you?"

"So-so." The judge made a gesture with his hand. "How is your son behaving? Is he being a good boy, doing what he's supposed to and not giving you any trouble?"

"Yes, your honor. He's doing much better."

Diego rolled his eyes. He wasn't doing better; he was as messed-up as ever.

"I'm glad he's behaving," Judge Ferrara said, for the first time smiling at Diego.

As Diego smiled back weakly, he recalled how the judge had told him he could speak for himself last time in court. If Ms. Delgado wasn't going to make his case, should he do it himself? No way. That would be truly crazy.

"Are you in agreement," the judge asked the prosecutor, "with Mr. Vidas's recommendation of restitution and SIS?"

"Yes, your honor," answered the prosecution.

Diego drew a deep gulp. If he was going to speak up, he had to do it soon.

"Counsel?" Judge Ferrara asked Ms. Delgado. "Have you discussed the recommendation with your client?"

Before she could answer, Diego raised his hand. "Um, excuse me, your honor, sir?"

The judge turned to him, as did every other person in the room. "You wish to say something?"

"Yes, your honor." Diego's voice quavered. His face felt like it was on fire.

The judge leaned back in his high-backed leather chair and folded his hands over his black robe. "Go ahead. What is it?"

Diego swallowed the lump beneath his tie. "I'd like to be on probation, sir."

The judge's eyebrows rose up from behind his glasses. "You *want* to be on probation?"

Diego nodded, too tense to speak. Instead he glanced warily at Vidas and found him staring back, looking a little bewildered.

"Well, this is a first," the judge mused. As though delighted, he addressed the room: "I've had parents, teachers, police, and victims ask me to put a boy on probation, but it's the first time I've ever been asked by the offender."

He returned his gaze to Diego. "And what makes you think you should be on probation?"

Diego thought carefully about how he might make the judge understand. He glanced at Vidas, whose look had turned stern.

"Because," Diego said, remembering their conversation, "my anger is dealing with me. And I don't know how to handle it . . . your honor."

Judge Ferrara stared back at him. Hard.

Diego felt himself weaken. Was he about to get yelled at in front of everybody?

After a minute, Judge Ferrara turned his gaze to Ms.

Delgado. "Did your client discuss this with you?"

Diego avoided looking at her, figuring she'd be mad, but her voice came out flat. "He mentioned probation, your honor, but I thought he'd misunderstood."

The judge looked across the courtroom. "Mr. Vidas, did he discuss it with you?"

Diego gripped his chair arms. Would Vidas be angry and tell the judge to send him to a shrink?

"He asked about probation," Vidas said. Although his voice sounded a little angry, his next words seemed to put the blame on himself. "But I didn't realize he felt so strongly about it, your honor."

Judge Ferrara's gaze traveled between Diego and Vidas. "Well, I don't think it's an offender's role to tell this court he should be on probation." His eyes narrowed at Diego, but then his voice softened. "On the other hand, it's definitely unusual for a boy to *ask* for probation. Mr. Vidas, could you handle one more case?"

Diego held his breath, recalling the stack of folders already on Vidas's desk.

"If that's the court's decision," Vidas said, "I can handle one more."

"Would you have any objection," Judge Ferrara asked Ms. Delgado, "if your client was placed on probation?"

"If he feels he needs it, your honor, I'd have no objection."

"Any objection?" the judge asked the prosecutor.

"No, your honor."

Judge Ferrara leaned back in his big leather chair and stared at Diego, continuing to deliberate in his mind. "Mr. Vidas, I'm going to yield to your discretion. Whatever you recommend, I'll sign off on. Would you please talk to the boy?"

"Yes, your honor. I'll do that."

"Next case," the judge announced. But he kept his eyes trained on Diego as he closed his file and handed it to the silver-haired clerk.

Diego stood, nervously bumping his foot on the table, and followed the others out of the court.

"Let me know what you decide," Ms. Delgado told Vidas in the waiting room. Then she turned to Diego. "Talk to Mr. Vidas about why you want to be on probation, okay? And no more surprises." She smiled at Diego's mom and patted her arm good-bye, explaining that she had to attend another case.

"I'd like to speak with him alone," Vidas told Diego's mom. His voice had a noticeable edge.

"Listen to what he tells you," his mom scolded Diego.

"I know," Diego replied, tugging anxiously at his necktie.

Like the last time they'd met, Vidas led Diego down the hallway into the cramped office. Except this time, he slammed the door closed. *Bam!*

Diego flinched.

"Don't you *ever*," Vidas said, stepping up to Diego's face, "pull a stunt like that again! If you have something to say to me, say it!"

I tried, Diego thought, but he felt too nervous to utter it aloud. He attempted to scoot back but had no room with the chair behind him.

"Do you hear me?" Vidas asked louder.

Diego didn't like him standing so close.

"Yeah," he sputtered, every muscle in his body fighting the urge to push Vidas away. "I guess I messed up."

"Damn right, you did!"

"No," Diego said, looking Vidas in the eye. "I mean I messed up by thinking I could talk to you."

"What?" Vidas tilted his head, perplexed.

Diego took a breath and collected his thoughts. "You told me unless I open up, nobody can help me, right?"

"Yeah," Vidas said guardedly. "That's right."

"You said," Diego continued, "I've got a lot to feel hurt and angry about because of people leaving me. Right?"

"That's right," Vidas repeated.

"Well, I tried to talk to you," Diego said, his throat tightening, "but it's like you want to ditch me too—just like everybody else."

Tears were brimming in Diego's eyes. He lifted his hand to his cheek and the cuff of his shirt rose up a little—enough for Vidas to notice.

His gaze fixed on Diego's wrist. "Let me see your arm."

Diego brought his hand back down, realizing his mistake. "Um, what for?"

Vidas ignored the question. "Unbutton your sleeve."

Diego hesitated, his mind a whirlwind. He'd never expected this to happen. How could he have been so stupid? Reluctantly, he lifted his arm, unbuttoned the cuff, and rolled up the sleeve, displaying the crisscross slashes.

Vidas's eyes widened. "Your other arm?"

Diego balked, a faint mist of perspiration beading on his forehead. Grudgingly, he unfastened the other cuff, exposing more scars.

Vidas shook his head in disbelief. "How far up do they go?"

Diego glanced away, not wanting to answer. The sweat rolled down his face.

"Unbutton your shirt," Vidas ordered.

"Why?" Diego protested. If Vidas tried to lay one finger on him, he'd deck him, even if he was his PO.

"I just want to see," Vidas said. "I'm not going to hurt you." He stepped back and sat down in his swivel chair to give Diego room.

Diego remained still. He didn't want Vidas to see his wounds. He wished he could bolt out the door. But then what? Not seeing any alternative, he slowly pulled his tie loose from his collar and let it drop onto the chair behind him. Gazing down at the carpet, he unbuttoned his shirt.

"My God!" Vidas exclaimed. "Who did that to you?"

To Diego, the question seemed strange. "I did it myself."

Vidas winced as if failing to understand.

Diego tugged on the elastic cord around his neck and held up the bone-colored shark's tooth, feeling suddenly emboldened. "I'll show you."

The impulse came unexpectedly; he'd never shown anybody how he did it. Pressing the tooth across his right forearm, a bright red stripe flooded from his skin.

"Stop it!" Vidas leaped up, pushing the tooth away. He

yanked a tissue from his desk and shoved it onto Diego's arm, staunching the blood flow. "Why didn't you tell me about this?"

The shock in Vidas's voice, usually so calm, surprised Diego—and he saw an opportunity. "Now will you put me on probation?"

Vidas glared at him. "I don't like being manipulated. Button your shirt—"

The phone rang, interrupting him. While Vidas answered, Diego closed his shirt. He hadn't meant to manipulate Vidas. Had he?

"Please tell the bailiff I'll be right there," Vidas said into the phone. But upon hanging up he stared at Diego, hesitating.

Diego glanced down at the carpet, ashamed and confused, wondering if Vidas would try to stop him by taking the tooth away. If he did, it wouldn't matter. Diego would use something else. Surely Vidas knew that.

"Sorry," he told Vidas softly, "if you think I'm manipulating you. Let me just ask you something, then I won't bother you anymore." As he spoke, his voice started to break. "You said I've got to find ways to connect with people other than with my fists, right?"

Vidas gazed back at him without answering.

"So how do I do that, Mr. Vidas? Can you tell me?"

The two faced each other across the stillness of the room. The phone jangled again and Vidas let it ring: once, twice, three times.

"Yes?" he finally answered. "I'm on my way." He picked up

a folder, telling Diego, "I've got to go. You should've told me about this earlier."

A curtain of silence hung between them as they stepped down the tile hallway to where the bailiff gestured impatiently at his watch. "The judge is waiting, Mr. Vidas."

Vidas turned to Diego. "I'll let you know what I decide." His voice revealed no clue. Then he disappeared into the court-room, leaving Diego standing in the hall.

CHAPTER 7

"WHAT HAPPENED?" Diego's mom asked. She'd waited for him in the court reception room, talking with another mom.

"Nothing happened," Diego grumbled and started toward the elevator. "Can we just go?"

He punched the down button and waited, wishing he'd never revealed his cuts to Vidas. He hadn't meant to admit all the things he'd said. Now he felt exposed and raw, like he wanted to crawl out of his skin and start life over as somebody different. Someone new.

Instead, he had to return to the same stupid school, put up with Guerrero's dumbass comments, fantasize about a girl he couldn't even manage a simple conversation with, and try to block from his mind memories and images that made him wish he were dead.

When he got home that afternoon, he slammed the door to his room, pulled off his shirt, and finished the slash he'd started in Vidas's office, wanting to forget about everything—

the world, his life, Mac. And for an instant, he did forget. But when the pain of the cut subsided, everything he'd forgotten came crashing back on him.

In geometry class later that week, Ms. Rainier was explaining tangent circles when a knock at the door interrupted her. After answering, she called into class: "Diego? Come to the hall, please."

As she resumed her lecture, Diego stood up, wondering: What was he in trouble for this time? He felt so nervous that he accidentally knocked the book off his desk. Fortunately, Kenny caught it for him.

When Diego got to the hallway, there stood Vidas. No doubt he'd come to inform him if he'd be on probation or not. In his hand, he held Diego's crimson-colored necktie. "You left this in my office the other day." Vidas handed him the tie.

"Thanks."

"How're you feeling?" Vidas asked.

"Um, okay. I guess." Diego fidgeted the tie into a circle, waiting.

"I gave the judge my recommendation," Vidas announced, his eyes fixed on Diego. "Congratulations, you've got six months probation."

"For real?" Diego asked, the tie slipping from his fingers.

"I want to see you in my office at four-thirty Thursday," Vidas answered.

"Got it." Diego nodded eagerly, picking up the tie. "Um, thanks."

"Don't thank me yet," Vidas said. His tone made Diego a

little nervous, but then he gave Diego a faint grin—enough to reassure him.

When he walked back into class, Kenny whispered, "Are you in trouble?"

"No." Diego sat down with a cheerful bounce. "The judge put me on probation."

After his last court date, Diego had explained to Kenny what had happened with Vidas. Now Kenny peered at him through his glasses. "Are you sure you've thought this through?"

"Yeah." Diego tossed his pencil into the air and caught it.

"Diego! Kenny!" Ms. Rainier called out. "Pay attention, please."

"I'm sure," Diego whispered to Kenny and tried to calm his excitement.

When he got home that afternoon, he phoned his mom and told her, "I got bad news: The judge put me on probation." He wasn't sure why he said it that way. Maybe he was having second thoughts and needed reassurance. Or perhaps he just wanted to get a reaction from her. Either way, it worked.

"That's *good* news," she argued. "Maybe now you'll learn to control your temper."

"Yeah," Diego said, happy with her response.

His good mood continued into the next day, when he saw Ariel at her locker. Ever since his last screw-up, he'd been hoping she might need his help with her books again or something. This time he was determined to be less of a blithering dork. Unfortunately, though, she was busy with her friends and didn't even look in his direction. Each day that followed, he waited—and hoped.

Two days later, a storm blew in from the Gulf with swirling gusts and pouring rain. When Diego got to school, he sprinted inside and was shaking the water off his jacket when Ariel suddenly ran in beside him, her face shimmering with raindrops.

The wind had blown her umbrella inside out and she struggled to fold it into place. Diego saw his chance. Shoving his sopping hair out of his eyes, he asked, "Can I, um, help you?"

"Oh, hi. Sure." She handed him the umbrella and smiled gently. "You seem to always be coming to my rescue."

"No problem." He grinned nervously and wrangled the thing into shape.

"Thanks," she said when he gave it back. Then they both stood there, staring at each other, while students jostled past.

"So, um . . ." Diego swallowed the knot in his throat. "Can we like, um, maybe hang out sometime? I mean, if you have a boyfriend, never mind. I understand."

"No, I don't have a boyfriend," she replied. "How about you? Are you seeing someone?"

"Me?" Her question floored him. Who on earth would he be seeing? "Um, no."

"All righty," she said. "Then I would like to hang out sometime."

A wave of amazement washed over him. Now what was he supposed to say?

"Are you always this shy?" she asked. Without waiting for an answer, she pulled a ballpoint from her jeans and reached for his hand to write her number on.

"Um, no, don't!" He moved his hand away, afraid she'd see his cuts.

"What's the matter? You ticklish?" She glanced toward his wrist and her face changed as if she'd noticed something.

"Here, write on this," he said, handing her a notebook from his backpack.

She gazed at him as if she wanted to ask a question. He tugged his jacket sleeves down, his arteries pulsing with panic and excitement.

To his relief, she didn't ask. Instead, she wrote down her phone number with a smiley drawn next to it. "Call me, okay?" She grinned slightly but her voice sounded serious.

"Um, sure. Thanks."

Had she spotted his cuts? Would she ask about them if he did call? How could they hang out without her discovering his scars and asking questions about him? How could anything possibly ever work out with her?

While she joined some friends, he headed toward his locker, thinking about what Vidas had told him: He was already in jail. A jail he was making for himself.

CHAPTER 8

"WHAT'S THAT FOR?" Vidas asked while he led Diego down the hall to their appointment.

In Diego's hand was a can of household oil that he'd rummaged out of the garage.

"For your chair," Diego explained. "So you won't have to hear it squeak."

Vidas smiled, bobbing his head as though impressed. "Great!"

Inside the cluttered office, they flipped the chair upside down and squeezed some oil into the swivel. After setting the chair right side up, Vidas sat down and rocked back and forth. No squeak.

"Thanks." He extended the candy jar from his desk out to Diego. This time, Diego took a candy.

"So"—Vidas set the jar back on his desk—"how're you feeling?"

"Fine," Diego said, eager to talk about Ariel.

"Fine is not a feeling," Vidas said and pointed to the smiley-face poster. "Pick one."

Diego smirked and almost picked *Annoyed*. But instead he chose the closest thing he could find to "fine."

"Glad, I guess."

"About anything in particular?" Vidas asked.

"Well . . ." He was eager to tell him about Ariel, but first: "Glad that you decided to put me on probation."

"Okay." Vidas gave an understanding nod. "To start us out, I've drawn up a treatment contract."

"A what?" Diego sat up in his seat. Nobody had ever mentioned a contract. "I thought we were just going to talk like before."

"First we need to set some rules." Vidas handed him a printed sheet. "I'd like you to read your copy aloud and we'll discuss it as we go along."

Diego shuffled his feet, uneasy. Although he'd figured there'd be rules, he'd never imagined they'd be in a written contract.

"'To comply with probation,'" he began reading, "'I agree to abide by the terms below. Number one: Absent a valid excuse such as illness, I will report to probation appointments on time.'"

"I want to meet with you once a week," Vidas explained. "I'll also phone your mom and drop by school to ask your teachers how you're doing. Any questions about that?"

"Nope." Diego relaxed a tiny bit. He could manage that.

The second item stated that he had to attend school

without unexcused absences. That was no problem; he never skipped classes. Quickly, he moved on to number three.

"'I agree to obey all reasonable and lawful commands of my parents and school officials. My curfew time to be home at night is nine p.m. Sunday through Thursday and ten p.m. Friday and Saturday.'" He glanced up at Vidas, frowning. "Are you serious? Nobody I know has to be home that early. No one."

"Then I guess," Vidas replied, "the people you know aren't on probation."

That wasn't exactly true; Guerrero was. But apparently he'd been ignoring his curfew. Diego shifted in his seat. This whole thing was starting to suck.

The next item stated that he wouldn't use or possess alcohol or any illegal drugs. He'd never liked the bitter taste of alcohol ever since Mac had given him his first sip. It made Diego cough. Mac laughed. Maybe that experience had turned Diego off from drinking. Or perhaps it was the smell of whiskey on Mac's breath. In any case, Diego wasn't interested in alcohol or drugs.

After that was an item about paying restitution for Fabio's hospital bill. Diego had hoped Vidas would forget about that.

Then he read the final item. "'I agree to be of good behavior and refrain from self-destructive activities, including cutting myself.'"

Diego stopped and stared at the words. What if he couldn't stop cutting? Would Vidas send him to juvie?

"What happens if I mess up?" he asked Vidas.

"Well," Vidas said, sounding as if he expected that might happen, "first you tell me about it. Then we discuss it. After that, depending on how bad you mess up, we talk about the consequences. The most important thing is for you to be honest with me. And with yourself. I can only help you if you're truthful."

Diego returned his gaze to the contract. A line marked *Parent/Guardian Signature* provoked a new worry. "But, um, my mom doesn't know I cut myself."

"You mean, she hasn't seen all that?" Vidas motioned to Diego's arms.

"No."

Vidas took a breath. "Then now you get to tell her."

Yeah, right. As though it were that simple.

"How do you fear she might react?" Vidas asked.

Diego's legs began to jiggle. "She'll probably tell me how difficult I make life for her. She acts as if everything I do is to get back at her."

"For what?"

"I don't know."

"Did she do something that hurt you?"

The question stopped Diego. *Had* his mom hurt him? "Well, she's never listened to me. She *never* listens."

At least not like this—sitting down and making time to hear what he had to say. Nobody had ever listened to him so closely, not even Kenny.

"If she were to listen to you," Vidas suggested, "what would you tell her?"

Diego was quiet a moment. "I'm not sure."

"In that case," Vidas said, "you can start by telling her about the cutting. Okay?"

Diego nodded, even though he had no idea how he'd do it.

"Great," Vidas said. "Sign both copies on the dotted line." He handed Diego the copy he'd been reading. "Take them home. After your mom signs them, keep one and bring one back to me."

Diego signed his name and folded the contracts into his pocket. Then he stared at Vidas. "So, um, can I talk to you about something else now?"

"You can talk to me about anything," Vidas said. "Anything at all."

"Well, um . . ." Diego faltered, trying to sort out his thoughts. "You know how you talked about people leaving?"

"Yes?"

"So . . ." Diego cleared his throat. "Do you think somebody who's had people leave them all their life can change . . . so that people don't keep leaving them?"

Vidas studied him for a long moment before responding. "Diego, your dad, your grandma, your stepdad . . . those people didn't leave because of anything you did. You know that, don't you?"

Diego gave a shrug, unconvinced. "So, do you think I can change?"

"Absolutely," Vidas said, his voice full of certainty. "You can deal with things that happened in the past. And you can change your behavior so you don't make people *want* to leave you in the future."

"So, like, if I met somebody . . ." Diego imagined Ariel smiling at him. "And, you know, because of problems I've had, that wouldn't . . ." His voice trailed off. He knew what he wanted to say; he just didn't know how to say it.

"There's somebody you like?" Vidas asked.

Diego felt his cheeks warm. "Yeah."

Vidas smiled a little. "Do you want to tell me about it?"

"Um, sure." Diego squirmed in his seat. "Like, what do you want to know?"

"What do you want to tell me?" Vidas asked.

"Well, her name's Ariel. She likes tropical fish, the same as me. But every time I try to talk to her I get all tongue-tangled."

Vidas nodded. "That happens to everyone."

"Not like to me," Diego argued.

"Well, it happens to me," Vidas replied.

"No way!" Diego found it hard to believe; Vidas seemed to always have a sense of calm and ease—except for that time he'd gotten angry.

"*Way!*" Vidas now insisted.

"So, like, what am I supposed to do?" Diego's voice grew agitated. "I don't know what to say to her."

"You can start by telling her that. Be honest. Relax. Girls often do more of the talking. Let her ask *you* questions. And keep breathing."

Diego took a breath, anxious at the mere idea of phoning

Ariel and even uneasier at the thought of her asking him questions. What if she found out the truth about him?

"You can do it," Vidas told him. "Trust yourself."

How do I do that? Diego thought. He was probably the person he trusted least on earth.

"Anything else you'd like to talk about today?" Vidas asked, glancing at his watch.

"Nope." That was enough—more than enough.

"Then for next week," Vidas said, standing up, "discuss the contract with your mom and bring me back a copy. Okay?"

Diego stood to leave, uncertain which worried him more: the prospect of calling Ariel or of talking with his mom.

After lunch on Sunday, his mom's day off, he helped to clear the table and load the dishwasher. Once Eddie had gone to play and was out of earshot, Diego told her, "You need to sign something for probation."

"What is it?" she asked, drying her hands with the dishcloth.

He handed her the contract and a pen. "Just sign at the bottom."

"Not so fast! I need to read it first." She sat down at the kitchen table and started to read. "This sounds great. It's good for you to have rules." But her brow furrowed as she got to the last item. "What does that mean, 'cutting' yourself?"

Diego leaned nervously against the counter. "Sometimes I, um, cut myself."

His mom shook her head, obviously not understanding. "You mean by accident?"

"Um, no." He fidgeted with the ends of his sleeves. "On purpose."

"On purpose?" Her entire face became a question mark. *"No comprendo."*

Not knowing how to explain it, he grasped a cuff and slowly slid it above his wrist. As the hatch work of cuts came into view, he watched his mom's face turn pale.

"You did that?" She stood up from the table and pushed the sleeve up his forearm, examining the slashes.

Diego withered with guilt. He'd known the sight would upset her.

"Take your shirt off," she told him.

Reluctantly, he pulled the long-sleeve tee over his head, revealing the pink and red scars across his arms and chest. She drew a sharp breath at the sight.

"How could you do this?" Her eyes filled with tears as she reached out and moved her fingertips gently across the swollen wounds. "You had such beautiful skin."

Her touch embarrassed him a little. It also made him feel close to her in a way he hadn't for a long time. Finally, he was getting the sympathy he'd longed for from her.

"Why didn't you tell me about this?" she said, teardrops spilling onto her cheeks.

"I figured you knew." The extent of her emotion surprised him. Had she truly never noticed or had she just turned a blind eye? She was his ma; she *should've* noticed. After all, Vidas had noticed. "I figured you didn't want to know."

She shot him a somber look. "You should have said something."

"Well, didn't you think it was sort of strange that I always wear long sleeves?" He pulled away from her and yanked his shirt back on, annoyed. "You never noticed because you don't care about me. You never have."

"Of course I care." She snapped a look at him. "You think it's easy being your mother? I've always taken care of you. Why do you think I work two jobs? And you repay me by getting into fights and cutting yourself!"

There it was: accusing him of trying to get back at her.

"I forbid you to do this anymore," she told him.

"It's *my* skin. I'll do what I want." He picked up the pen and slammed it onto the table. "Just sign the form."

"Don't talk to me that way!"

"I'll talk to you any damn way I want!"

"I'm going to tell Mr. Vidas," his mom said.

"Tell him! I don't care. There are things I can tell him too, you know." His fists began to curl. He had to get away before he did something he'd regret.

He stormed to his room, slammed the door, and rammed his fist through the wall. Pain seared through his knuckles, overpowering his anger. As he withdrew his hand from the plasterboard, he shook his fingers out. His fist hurt like crazy. But at least he'd only punched a wall.

CHAPTER 9

THE FOLLOWING MORNING, Diego found both copies of the probation contract lying on the kitchen counter, signed by his mom.

"Good morning," she told him while tending to Eddie's breakfast.

"Morning," he grumbled back, his anger still smoldering.

"Do you want to see a doctor?" she asked, gazing toward his arms—and the cuts beneath his sleeves.

"Are you sick?" Eddie asked him.

"No," Diego told both of them. "I'm fine." His mom's sudden concern annoyed him. Why hadn't she paid as much attention to him before, when Mac was alive? He wolfed down his breakfast and left for school, eager to take his mind off of home.

As he approached his locker, he spotted Ariel across the hallway with her friends. Seeing him, she waved hi. He waved back, kind of embarrassed that he still hadn't worked up the nerve to call her.

For the remainder of the day, he repeated over and over in his mind the advice Vidas had given him: Relax. *Trust yourself. Be honest. Keep breathing. You can do it.*

That evening after dinner, while Eddie watched TV, Diego carried the phone to his room. Trembling a little, he opened his notebook to the page with Ariel's number. Buoyed by the smiley she'd drawn, he dialed.

When she answered, he swallowed hard, trying to quench his suddenly parched throat. "Um, hi. This is Diego. You know, from school?"

"I know," she said cheerily. "I recognize your voice."

He assumed she meant she didn't like it. "I don't like it either. Sounds like a frog."

"No, it doesn't," she protested. "I like it. It sounds mature."

Mature? Nobody had ever described his voice as mature. She must be joking.

"I like *your* voice," he told her, not just being nice; he meant it.

"Thanks. So, what are you up to?"

"Um, calling you." He switched the phone to his other hand to wipe the sweat from his palm. "You told me to, remember?"

"Of course. I was wondering when you would." She gave a soft laugh. "You're funny."

"Um, I am?" He liked that he could make her laugh. Maybe he wasn't as depressing as he thought. "So, like, um . . ." He realized he should ask her something before she started asking *him* questions. "So, um, how're your fish? You bought neon tetras, right?"

"Wow, you remember that?"

"Yeah . . ." He felt himself turning neon red. "Tetras are a good choice for freshwater aquariums. They tend to be peaceful and hardy."

"So far they're great," Ariel agreed. "How about you? Do you have any fish?"

"Saltwater ones," he explained and told her about his clownfish and gobies. Then they got to talking about classes and school. Actually, *she* did most of the talking, like Vidas had predicted. To his relief, she didn't ask about Mac's suicide or anything really personal. Maybe she *hadn't* spotted his cuts. And all the while Diego kept reminding himself: *Breathe!* When he glanced at the clock, he was amazed to find half an hour had passed.

"So, um," he asked, "do you really want to hang out sometime?"

"Yeah," she replied. "How about this weekend?"

Diego's throat abruptly clamped up. Had she really said 'yeah'?

"Um, I work Saturdays. How about Sunday?" His mom didn't work Sunday. He could ask to borrow the car.

"Sunday would be great," Ariel replied. "What do you want to do?"

"Do you like the aquarium?" Diego asked. The Texas State Aquarium was his second favorite place in town, the beach being first.

"I love the aquarium." Ariel's voice rang with enthusiasm.
"Awesome! It's a date."

The word "date" echoed in his mind. His first date. Ever. The phone nearly slipped out of his hands.

"We can talk more before then," she continued, "but now I've got to get back to homework. Thanks for calling."

After hanging up, Diego stared into space, a little dazed. Had he actually booked a date with—to his mind—the most amazing girl at school, perhaps even in the entire universe? A flash of excitement surged up from his toes, through his body, and erupted in a thunderous whoop.

THURSDAY AFTERNOON, Diego arrived early for his appointment, excited to tell Vidas about the phone call with Ariel. He said hi to the receptionist and was just sitting down when Vidas stepped out of the elevator, carrying a paper bag.

"Hi, Diego. Come on back. I just went to fetch some lunch. Had cases all day."

Inside the office, Vidas hung up his blazer. After plopping into his swivel chair, he tucked the ends of his necktie into his shirt's front pocket and pulled a sandwich from the paper bag. "You want half? It's tuna fish."

"No, thanks." It would feel too weird to eat half of his PO's sandwich.

"At least take some chips." Vidas tossed Diego a pack. "I bought an extra."

"All right." Diego caught the bag. "Thanks."

"So, how're you feeling?" Vidas asked, and bit into his sandwich.

"Great!" Diego announced, opening the chips. "I did it."

"Did what?"

"Phoned Ariel. And like you said, I kept breathing."

"Ah. Good! How'd it go?"

"Um, okay, I guess. We're going to the aquarium Sunday. On a date."

"A date!" Vidas exclaimed. "I knew you could do it. How do you feel about it?"

"Nervous. Like, what am I supposed to do?"

"Same as before," Vidas said, lifting his sandwich. "Relax. Breathe. Just be yourself."

Diego shook his head. He didn't want to be himself. He wished he could be someone else. Somebody confident, cool, normal.

"I don't get it. She could have practically any guy she wants. So, why's she interested in *me*?"

Vidas swallowed his mouthful. "Could you ask her?"

"I guess so." Diego would never have thought of that.

As Vidas raised his sandwich again, a chunk of tuna spilled out onto the top part of his tie. "Oh, man!" He put his sandwich down, pulled off his tie, and stared at the mayonnaise stain. "I ruin at least one a month." He opened a desk drawer, took out a stain stick, and rubbed the spot.

Diego watched him. "Why don't you just take it off when you eat?"

"Yeah, I should, shouldn't I?" Before taking another bite, Vidas asked, "So, what about the contract and your mom?"

Diego stopped eating his chips and sat stiffly in his chair. He'd forgotten it.

"Um, she read and signed it. I swear she did. But I forgot to bring your copy. I can bring it tomorrow if you want."

"Tomorrow is good," Vidas said calmly. "Just leave it with Mrs. Ahern. So tell me: How'd your mom react?"

"Um . . ." Diego crumpled up his chip bag and lobbed it into the trash. "Fine . . . until the part about the cutting . . . When I showed her, she got kind of upset."

"What do you mean?" Vidas pitched his crumpled sandwich wrapper toward the wastebasket, actually making it in.

"Well, first she started to cry. Then she got angry. And then . . . I kind of blew up at her."

Vidas nodded and chewed on his chips. "What made you angry?"

Diego thought a moment. "Because . . . she acted like she'd never noticed the cuts. But how could she *not* have noticed? *You* noticed. And then she acted like I did it just to get back at her. So then . . . I punched another hole in the wall."

Vidas glanced at Diego's fist. "That must've hurt."

"Yeah." Diego ran his fingers across his knuckles. "But at least I didn't punch *her*."

Vidas stopped chewing his chips and his voice came out concerned: "Have you ever hit her?"

"No. But I was afraid I might."

Vidas pondered that before taking another chip. "So instead of hurting her you hurt yourself."

Diego hadn't thought of it that way.

"Do you think," Vidas asked, "maybe that's part of why you cut yourself? In place of hurting other people?"

Diego shifted his feet on the carpet. "I don't know." All he knew for certain was that when the anger consumed him, he had to do something to let it out.

"Have you cut yourself," Vidas asked, crumpling his empty chip bag, "since you signed the contract last week?"

"No," Diego replied truthfully.

"What's it feel like," Vidas probed deeper, "when you do cut yourself?"

Diego gave a shrug. "Good."

"*Good?*" Vidas winced. "Doesn't it hurt?"

"Yeah," Diego explained, "but it's a good hurt—a rush. For a second, it's the only thing you feel. Like a high. Everything else disappears."

"What disappears?" Vidas asked. "What *don't* you want to feel?"

"I don't know. Everything." As Diego's legs began to jiggle, he gazed down at his tattered sneakers. Last week, he'd asked his mom for a new pair and she'd told him he had to wait. There was never enough money since Mac's death.

Vidas was saying something. Diego glanced up from the carpet. "Um, sorry. I spaced out. What did you say?"

"I asked when did you first start to cut yourself?"

Diego hesitated and folded his arms across his chest. "I guess after Mac died."

Vidas raised his eyebrows. "So, Mac committed suicide and you started to hurt yourself? It sounds like maybe there's a connection. What do you think?"

"Why do we always have to talk about him?"

"Because, one, he was your stepdad, and two, he committed suicide. That's a pretty major event in your life."

Diego turned to look out the window at the harbor. In the distance a tiny tugboat was pulling some huge ship across the channel.

"How did he get along with your mom?" Vidas asked, his voice steady.

"Fine."

"'Fine' doesn't tell me much," Vidas pressed him. "How often did they fight? Once a month? Once a week? Every night?"

Diego recalled how at first Mac and his mom hadn't fought at all. But after moving to America, the arguments started—about money or Mac's drinking or stupid small stuff. Diego would retreat to his room, but Mac never allowed him to have a lock on the door. Diego had complained about it to his mom, but she wouldn't listen.

"Maybe a couple of times a week," Diego answered Vidas.

"Did he ever hit her?"

"Nope."

"Did he ever hit you?"

"No." Mac had never even spanked him. He never needed to.

"Did he ever," Vidas continued, "try to touch you . . . in a way you thought was inappropriate, that made you uncomfortable?"

"No!" Diego sat up in his chair, his cheeks reddening, his head burning. "Why do you keep asking stuff like that?"

"Because," Vidas said, "sometimes that happens in families. And nobody talks about it. The person it happens to is left stuck with their feelings—hurt and anger. What they don't talk out, they end up acting out."

Diego turned away, refusing to look at Vidas. He suddenly wished he'd never asked for probation. What had he been thinking?

"If Mac did anything like that to you, it wasn't your fault. You know that, don't you? You don't need to feel ashamed or guilty."

"I don't!" Diego clenched the arms of his chair, restraining the urge to bolt from the room. "I've got nothing to feel guilty or ashamed about."

"I agree," Vidas replied. "That's what I said."

Their eyes met and held for a moment, then Diego shifted his gaze out the window again, trying to calm himself. "Nothing happened."

"Okay," Vidas said a soothing voice. But then he added, "If it did, I hope one day you'll tell me. So, what are you feeling right now?"

"Like I want to get out of here." Every muscle in his body was straining to keep him seated.

"Do you feel angry?" Vidas asked.

"Yeah."

"Can you say that?"

Diego flashed his eyes at him. "I'm angry!"

Vidas gave a nod. "It's good when you can state your anger. You don't have to punch someone, or cut yourself, or put your fist through a wall. You can just say, 'I'm angry.'"

Diego knew that; he wasn't stupid. But when the rage

ignited, he forgot it. Like the cutting, rage was a high that made everything else fade away.

"What are you thinking?" Vidas asked.

"Nothing." Diego sat in silence, waiting for Vidas to ask or say something else. But Vidas remained quiet, until Diego couldn't stand it anymore.

"Are we done?" he asked.

Vidas slowly let out a sigh. "Is there anything else you want to talk about today?"

"No," Diego muttered. He just wanted to get out of here.

"Then you'll drop your contract off tomorrow?" Vidas asked and stood up.

"Yeah," Diego grumbled, and followed him out the office door.

When they got to the end of the hallway, Vidas gave him a pat on the shoulder. "See you next—"

"Don't touch me!" Diego whirled around, fists clenched.

Vidas sprang back, his eyes wide with alarm, arms raised to protect himself. "Whoa, easy! Take a breath. Stop and think."

Diego gulped a huge breath, adrenaline pumping through his body. Had he actually almost punched his PO? It wasn't his fault. Why did Vidas have to touch him? "I don't like it when you touch me!"

"I understand," Vidas said. He didn't sound angry, and yet how could he not be? "Take it easy. Keep breathing."

Diego breathed deep and let his fists drop. Why had he lashed out like that? Obviously, Vidas hadn't meant anything inappropriate by patting him on the back.

"I'm sorry," Vidas said, lowering his hands. "I won't do it again. You can tell me if I do something you don't like."

Diego lowered his gaze, ashamed and angry with himself. Would he ever stop losing control?

"You're opening up a lot of feelings," Vidas continued, his voice regaining its familiar calm. "Hang in there. Okay?"

Diego nodded, but he couldn't bring himself to look at Vidas. It was too scary to think what would've happened if he'd punched him.

Upon leaving the courthouse, instead of biking home he headed to the beach. From atop a dune, he stared at the surf, watching wave after wave roll in. He thought over the things he'd talked about with Vidas, and the things he *hadn't* talked about. The things he'd never told anyone—and never could.

As he leaned back, his elbows sank into the sand and the shark's tooth pressed against his chest. He sat up again, pulled the triangle from beneath his shirt, and turned it over between his fingers. He knew that if he cut himself he'd have to tell Vidas about it, but at least for now, the pain he was feeling would leave him.

He rolled up his sleeve and brought the tooth to his forearm. The tip pricked his skin, its pain immediate. A bright red bubble appeared, shimmering in the afternoon light like a setting sun. He sliced the tooth's serrated edge across his arm and watched the blood seep into a tiny trough. And for a moment, all his other anguish flowed away.

CHAPTER 11

THE FOLLOWING DAY AFTER SCHOOL, Diego rode his bike to the courthouse to drop off his probation contract, hoping he wouldn't see Vidas. He wasn't ready to admit that he'd cut himself.

He rushed in and out of the reception room as fast as possible, quickly handing Mrs. Ahern the contract, and raced all the way back to his neighborhood.

For dinner that evening he made ravioli. Then he did homework while debating how best to ask his mom for the car for his date.

In the days since their blow-up over the contract, he'd kept his distance from her. But tonight when she leaned into his bedroom doorway, he greeted her with a smile. "Hi, how was your day?"

"My day was okay," she said slowly, suspiciously. "Nothing special. How'd it go with Eddie tonight?"

"Fine. He brought you a painting he made in school. You want me to heat up some ravioli for you?"

"Sounds good." She nodded as if grateful for his improved mood. "Thanks."

While she changed from her work clothes, he put a plate of ravioli in the microwave and set a place for her at the kitchen table, next to Eddie's painting.

"What do you want to drink?" he asked as she shuffled in, wearing her slippers and nightgown.

"Just ice water, *mi amor*." She sat down to the plate of steaming ravioli and while he served her the water, she studied his face. "So, what's up?"

"Huh?" he asked, fiddling with the dishcloth. "What's up with what?"

"You know what." She gestured to the ravioli and ice water.

Diego sat down opposite her, paused to think, and decided to just go ahead and tell her. "Um, I need to use the car on Sunday to go to the aquarium."

She blew on the ravioli to cool it before answering, "Can you take Eddie?"

Diego cringed. Although he loved his little brother, he hadn't counted on having to bring him along. "Um . . . I can't. It's a date."

"A *date*?" His mom grabbed her ice water. "You mean with a girl?"

Diego leaned back. "No, with a broom."

His mom ignored his sarcasm. "With what girl?"

"Her name's Ariel." Diego shifted his feet. "Look, can I use the car or can't I?"

"Why are you getting so angry?" his mom asked.

"Because I don't want to talk about her."

"Well, I want to know about her. You've never been on a date before."

"So? You think I don't know that? Stop treating me like a kid."

"I'm not! I just didn't expect it, that's all."

"Why? You don't think a girl would want to go out with me?"

"Diego, why do you have to take everything I say the wrong way?"

"Forget it! I don't want the car."

"Diego, stop it! Yes, you can use the car. But I'd like to meet her sometime, okay?"

No way, Diego thought. She'd probably just embarrass him.

He returned to his room and resumed his homework, trying to forget about his mom. After all, she'd agreed to let him use the car. And soon the words in his book began to blur as his imagination leaped forward to his date . . . and Ariel.

On Saturday after work, he got a haircut at Cheap Cuts in the mall. Afterward, he wasn't exactly thrilled with how he looked, but at least his hair was neater. He spent most of Sunday morning getting ready—shaving the fuzz from his chin; clipping his nails; combing his hair, first to one side, then the other . . . After lunch he flossed and brushed and asked for the car keys.

"Are you bringing her something?" his mom replied.

In fact, Diego had thought of taking Ariel some flowers, but then decided that was too corny.

"A girl always likes if you bring her something," his mom
insisted.

"Like what?"

His mom hunted through the kitchen cupboards. "Here, take her these."

"*Gummy bears?*" Diego made a face. He'd never heard of anybody taking gummies to a date.

"It's the thought." His mom pressed the bag into his hand. "She'll appreciate it. You'll see."

He wasn't convinced but kept the bag anyway. While his mom searched her handbag for the car keys, she asked, "Does this girl know you're on probation?"

The question hit Diego like a splash of cold water. "Um, I'm not sure."

"She'd probably want to know." His mom held out the car keys. "Promise to tell her?"

Diego balked. Why did his mom always have to ruin everything? But he knew she was probably right.

"Okay!" He clenched his fist around the keys and hurried out the door before she could say anything else.

Ariel lived far on the other side of school, in a townhouse with a white alabaster sea horse out front. Diego forgot the gummy bag in the car and walked nervously up the driveway, his legs wobbling like jelly. Inside the house, dogs yapped excitedly. He rang the doorbell and waited, checking himself in the reflection of the window and combing a hand through his hair.

When the door opened, the sight of Ariel made him catch his breath. Like him, she'd gotten her hair cut too—not much, just enough to show her face more, making her look cuter than ever. Two dogs were wagging and panting at her feet.

"Hi. Don't mind them. This one's Neptune. We rescued him from the pound. And that's Pluto. The neighbors moved and left him. Come on in. My mom wants to meet you."

Diego followed Ariel inside, bravely putting one foot in front of the other. Although he'd figured he might have to meet her mom or dad, he'd hoped he wouldn't.

Her mom was in the kitchen watering plants. She looked like an older version of Ariel—chubby and a little faded, but with the same twinkling green eyes and warm smile. "It's nice to meet you," she said, shaking Diego's hand. "Ariel told me you're in the same grade. Do you live nearby?"

"Um, sort of." He told her where he lived and she remarked, "That's a nice area."

"Your house is nice too," he answered, not knowing what else to say, and shoved his hands in his pockets.

"Well, have a good time," she said and went back to watering the plants.

At the car, Diego remembered to open Ariel's door for her. When he climbed into the seat on the driver's side, she was holding the bag of multicolored gummies. "Can I have one?"

"Um, yeah." He started the engine, glad his mom had suggested them. "They're for you."

"Really? Thanks." Ariel opened the bag and held out a little green bear. "Want one?"

He nodded and opened his palm. For an instant her fingertips brushed his hand, sending little heat flashes pulsing through his body. Quickly, he pulled onto the road.

"I like your haircut," she told him.

"Um, thanks. I like yours."

"Yeah? You don't think it's too short?" She flipped down the visor mirror to check herself.

"No, it looks great. Everything about you, um . . . looks great."

"Thanks." She handed him an orange gummy. "I just got this shirt yesterday."

He'd noticed it looked new. But he thought she looked amazing no matter what she wore. That's what he meant when he said, "You'd look great even without clothes on."

His heart stopped as he realized how bad that sounded.

"Boy!" Ariel burst out laughing. "You move fast, don't you?"

"I'm, I'm sorry," he stammered. "I just meant . . . you're beautiful."

"You haven't seen me when I wake up." She laughed—a bright, sunny laugh. "Or you'd run away screaming."

"No, I wouldn't," he assured her. "But you would if you saw me."

"I don't think so," she said quietly, pressing another gummy into his hand.

When they arrived at the aquarium he paid for their entrance tickets—despite Ariel's protests—using the few bucks he'd had left after paying restitution, plus some money Kenny had loaned him.

They began their visit walking though the Amazon exhibit, looking at the thirteen-foot anaconda, the spike-toothed piranhas, and the huge hairy tarantula, big as a man's hand. At the sight of it, Ariel grabbed hold of Diego's arm, making his heart spring against his chest.

For the bottlenose dolphin show, the crowd had to squeeze together in the stands, but Diego didn't mind. Not one bit. The touch of Ariel's hip and shoulder pressing against his was far more thrilling than anything the dolphins did.

He hoped the bird-and-animal show would be equally packed. Unfortunately, it wasn't. The announcer asked for a volunteer to feed the anteater on stage, and Ariel raised her hand. When she got picked, Diego marveled at her bravery. He hated to get in front of groups. But she just laughed while the anteater slurped its long thin tongue across her hand and into the water bottle.

Next, Diego led her to his favorite exhibit, the huge aquarium that gave an underwater view of oil rig–type reefs in the Gulf of Mexico.

They wandered slowly past the tank's windows, and Ariel's hand kept brushing his. Was she doing it on purpose? Each time their fingers bumped, another little jolt of electricity zapped through his body.

Stepping close to the glass to peer at the eels and sharks, he summoned his nerve and slowly interlaced his fingers—one after another—between hers. It was his first time to ever hold a girl's hand in a romantic way. Her palm was soft and tender. And his was sweaty. *Very* sweaty.

Trying to think of something to say, he asked, "Do you ever dream about sharks?"

"No, why?" Her eyes blinked with curiosity. "Do you?"

"Um, yeah." He'd never mentioned it to anybody except Kenny.

"That must be scary," she replied.

"Yeah, it can be." Without realizing it, he grasped her hand a little tighter. "Sometimes I wake up; it seems so real."

Ariel gave his hand a squeeze. "Maybe we shouldn't be looking at sharks."

"It's okay," Diego said, worried that he may have scared her. "Actually, I like looking at them. I can watch them for hours."

"Maybe that's why you have nightmares." Ariel laughed.

He laughed too, wishing he could stay there forever, watching the sharks behind the glass, holding Ariel's hand, talking, and laughing.

When it came time to drive her home, a wave of sadness flowed over him. He liked her so much and wanted her to like him. But what would happen when he told her about probation? The question had been weighing on his mind all afternoon. He knew he had to tell her. She was bound to find out somehow. Better to hear it from him.

"I had a really great time," he said, parking in her driveway. "You have no idea how great."

"Me too," she answered. The afternoon sun was making her eyes sparkle with little flecks of light.

"So, um, I need to tell you something," Diego confessed, gripping the steering wheel for courage. "Um, I'm on court probation . . . for punching a guy."

He waited, staring ahead at the garage, worried that she'd leave now and never go out with him again.

"I know," she responded.

"You do?" He turned to her. She didn't look shocked at all.

"My friends told me." A faint smile tugged at the corners of her lips. "Some of them think you're kind of sketchy."

But if she knew, then why had she gone out with him? Why hadn't she mentioned it?

As if reading his mind, she continued, "I was waiting to see if you'd tell me."

"Well, I guess I was scared," he explained quickly, "that . . . you know . . . you wouldn't want to go out with me. . . . I'm sorry."

"That's okay." She gave an understanding shrug. "I'm glad you're being honest now."

He regretted that he hadn't told her sooner. She took hold of his hand between hers, praying-like, and in his excitement he forgot about the cuts.

"Are you going to tell me about those, too?" she asked, tracing her fingertip beneath the cuff of his long-sleeve shirt.

His entire body went tense. When had she noticed? What should he tell her? Now he was certain to lose her. "Um, sometimes I . . . Sometimes I cut myself."

"Why?" she asked, pushing his sleeve up to examine the scars.

"I don't know. To take my mind off my problems."

She stared at him, waiting for him to say more. "Problems like what?"

He hesitated, feeling like he was getting pulled in over his head. "Well, um . . . my life has been kind of complicated. I don't think you really want to hear it."

"Complicated like how?" she asked gently.

"Well, like . . ." The blood was thudding in his temples. "There are things you don't know about me, stuff that's hard to talk about, things in my past."

"You mean like your stepdad's suicide?"

"Yeah." He cringed, embarrassed and ashamed. "Stuff like that." He stared out the windshield, wishing he'd had a different life, one in which he wouldn't have to deal with all that had happened. "I just want to be normal, that's all."

"And what's normal?" Ariel said.

"I don't know, but I know it's not me." In order to prevent her from asking any more, he decided to ask her a question instead.

"Um, can I ask you something? If you knew all this stuff about me, why'd you go out with me?"

"Because," Ariel said, tenderly moving her fingers across his wrist. "You're shy . . . you're sweet . . . and because . . . it's like there's something hurt inside you that's calling out to me. I don't know how to explain it. I'm a little sketchy too, you know?"

"No, you're not!" He gave his head a vigorous shake. "You're like . . . perfect!"

"Perfect?" Her lips curled into a smile. "Hardly. There's stuff in my past that's hard for me to talk about too."

He stared at her, surprised. What stuff did she mean? It couldn't be as bad as his stuff. Could it?

"Well," he said. "If you ever want to . . . you know . . . talk about it, I can listen."

"Okay," she told him. "Maybe next time we can both talk more."

Next time? After all she knew about him, she actually wanted a next time?

He gazed nervously across the seat at her. The sunlight through the windshield played off her eyelashes as she gazed back at him. Was she wanting what he wanted?

Hesitantly, he tilted toward her, bringing his mouth halfway. And there she met him, her lips gently pressing his. They were kissing, just like he'd imagined. Her mouth was soft and tender. And her breath tasted sweet as gummy bears.

When they finally pulled apart, she gave him a long steady look that he didn't exactly understand. He knew what he wanted it to mean, but he wasn't certain that's what she meant.

"Thanks for a really nice time," she said. "See you at school tomorrow." And then she was walking up the sidewalk to her door, waving and smiling.

As he slowly drove home, he thought about their kiss and how perfect the entire afternoon had been. Maybe—just maybe—he could be normal after all.

DIEGO COULD HARDLY WAIT for his next appointment with Vidas, eager to report on his date with Ariel. Before leaving home he grabbed a bag of caramels his mom had bought, and when he got to Vidas's office, he pulled the bag from his backpack.

"They're for your jar," he told Vidas. "It's getting low."

"Great, thanks." Vidas filled the jar and listened attentively while Diego told him all about his date—everything except their kiss. That was too personal.

"She sounds like a nice girl," Vidas commented.

"*Nice?* She's more than just *nice*. She's amazing!"

"And apparently she likes you," Vidas added.

"Don't know why," Diego replied, even though she'd told him why.

"You were honest with her," Vidas offered. "That's a good thing. You told her you're on probation and let her know about your cuts."

"Yeah, I told her about probation because my mom *made*

me promise and about my cuts because she'd noticed them. I didn't *want* to, I *had* to."

"But you did it," Vidas argued. "Give yourself some credit. And you paid for her aquarium ticket. That was generous."

Diego hadn't thought of it as generous. He did it because he liked her—and he wanted her to like him.

"Now, come on," Vidas persisted. "Name at least one other thing she might like, something you like about yourself."

It amazed Diego how easily Vidas could come up with good stuff about him. When he tried to look inside himself, all he saw was the bad stuff. He took a breath and in a low voice confessed to Vidas, "I cut myself again."

Why he admitted it, he wasn't exactly sure. He could have kept it to himself. Vidas would never know.

"When?" Vidas asked, sounding curious, not angry.

"Um, right after our last meeting."

Vidas thought for a moment, as if attempting to recall what they'd talked about.

"Are you mad at me?" Diego asked.

"No, but I'm concerned. I don't want you to hurt yourself, Diego."

Diego slumped down in his seat, kind of wishing Vidas *would* be angry. Anger gave him something to fight against. Concern made him feel hopeless. "So, what's going to happen to me?"

"That's largely up to you," Vidas said.

"Are you going to send me to jail?"

"No."

"But what if I can't stop cutting?"

"I believe you can stop. But you've got to believe it too. You need to believe in yourself."

Diego slipped a little farther down in his chair. How could he believe in himself when he kept screwing up over and over? He felt as though he was sinking, and neither Vidas nor anybody else could save him.

"What if I asked you to hand over your shark's tooth?" Vidas said. "Would that stop you?"

Diego shook his head. He didn't want to let go of the tooth. "I'll just use something else," he told Vidas, expecting an argument.

But Vidas didn't argue. He sat silently, seeming to consider what else he could say.

While Diego waited, he glanced out the window. Several sailboats were tacking across the bay. The sight made him think about his dream—the nightmare. What if he told Vidas about the shark? He'd probably think Diego was crazy. What if he *was* crazy?

"Do you, um, know anything about dreams? Like what they mean?"

"I'm no expert," Vidas said. "But if you've had one you want to tell me, maybe we can figure it out together."

"Well"—Diego sat up in his chair—"I keep having this dream . . . where I'm stranded in the middle of the ocean, all alone, being pulled by a current toward this shark that's coming at me. It seems so real."

He paused to swallow and Vidas asked, "What happens?"

"The shark charges at me. Then there's a gunshot. And I wake up. . . . What do you think it means?"

Vidas scratched his chest a moment while thinking. "Dreams sometimes express feelings about our waking life. You said the dream starts with you stranded, all alone. Do you ever feel that way in real life?"

"Yeah." Even when he was with other people he often felt alone, like no one really knew him. He sometimes thought that if he died, it wouldn't make any difference. Nobody would care. His whole existence was pointless.

"In your dream," Vidas continued, "you say you're caught in a current. Maybe in real life you feel like you've gotten caught up in something you can't stop."

"Like cutting myself?" Diego asked. He figured that's what Vidas was getting at.

"Could be," Vidas said. "Or maybe whatever is beneath your cutting, the pain that's pulling at you."

Diego shifted in his seat. "And what about the shark?"

"Well . . ." Vidas pursed his lips. "What do you feel when it comes after you?"

"Terrified. What would you feel?"

"Terrified," Vidas agreed. "Have you ever felt that scared in real life?"

Diego's mind flashed to the night in the fishing boat with Mac, trying to get away, with nowhere to go. He'd been stranded.

"No," he told Vidas, not wanting to talk about Mac again.

"Never?" Vidas peered across the office at him.

Diego shuffled his feet. "What do you think the shark means?"

Vidas continued staring a moment before finally releasing a sigh. "It could be lots of things. . . . Feelings swimming around inside you, beneath the surface . . . Fear. Rage . . . It might be that destructive part of you. . . . Or maybe it's something in your past, pursuing you, eating at you. . . . A shark is a predator, an attacker. You mentioned a gunshot. Were there times you were around a gun? Mac's gun?"

"No." Diego glanced away, recalling the night before the suicide, in his room with Mac.

Vidas leaned forward in his chair. "Like I said before, Diego, whatever he did wasn't your fault. You don't need to protect him."

Diego clenched his jaw as images of Mac flooded into his mind: Mac shuffling into his bedroom at night, waking him, his hot breath, smelling of cigarette smoke and whiskey . . . Even though he'd torn Mac out of all those photos, his face still haunted him, perfectly clear, hollow-eyed, smiling, wanting him.

"Protect him from what?" Diego asked. "He's dead."

"Protect him from the truth," Vidas answered. "Maybe you're afraid the truth might hurt your family. Or perhaps you're scared of what you think it would say about you."

It almost seemed as if Vidas already somehow knew what had happened with Mac. But how could he know? And if he did, why didn't he just say so?

"Sometimes," Diego replied, "it feels like a shark is really out there somewhere, waiting for me. Do you think that's crazy?"

"No," Vidas said. "People stay with us after they die, through the things they said and did. Even though Mac's dead, to you he's still alive."

A chill passed through Diego as he thought about the part of the dream he hadn't told Vidas: of Mac's body bearing down on him.

"What else do you want to tell me?" Vidas asked.

"Nothing," Diego lied. He wished that Vidas would press him harder, somehow force him to talk. But Vidas kept silent, staring across the room at him for what seemed like forever.

"Okay," Vidas said at last. "I'm glad you told me about your cutting. Promise you'll tell me if you cut yourself again?"

"Sure, but . . . aren't you going to, like, punish me?"

"It seems to me you're already punishing yourself. Punishing you more isn't going to make you stop. Is it?"

Diego stared at him, not knowing what to answer.

Vidas stood and arched his back, stretching. "And thanks for telling me about that dream. I'll walk you down the hall."

Diego remained in his chair, feeling a sudden urge to tell Vidas everything—all that had happened. But how could he? It would be like reliving it.

Vidas glanced down at him. "You want to talk more?"

"No." Overcoming the urge, Diego quickly stood up.

When they got to the reception room, Diego recalled the previous time when Vidas had promised not to touch him again. True to his word, this time there was no pat on the back. Although Diego knew he should feel glad, instead he missed it.

CHAPTER 13

THE FOLLOWING MORNING Diego arrived at school early, like he had every day since his date with Ariel. While waiting for her, he organized his locker, shuffling books and arranging pens, until she appeared across the hallway.

He smiled and waved, wanting to ask, *When can we go out again?* Instead, he ended up exchanging inconsequential conversation about their fish and teachers and classwork. And when the bell rang, his heart gave a pang as he watched her walk away.

On Saturday, he biked to work as usual and spent the day stocking shelves and helping customers. The following day it rained, so instead of going to the beach, he and Kenny went to a movie—an action pic that Diego enjoyed but that Kenny thought was kind of gore-heavy. Afterward, they grabbed some pizza at the mall food court.

They'd just finished eating when Kenny announced, "Hey, there's Guerrero."

He was ambling through the crowd with Gomez, one of his buddies, and three girls with mascara-fringed eyes whom Diego had never seen before. *They must go to a different school,* he figured.

"Should we say hi?" Kenny asked, sounding a little worried.

"Nah, I better get home. I've got curfew, remember?"

"Oh, yeah." Kenny nodded as if relieved.

Guerrero almost walked past without noticing them, but then he glanced in their direction and shouted, "Yo, guys!" as though they were best friends.

"Now, if he starts anything," Kenny whispered, "just ignore him. Okay?"

"Yeah, I know." Diego chewed the ice remaining from his Coke as Guerrero led his group over to the table.

"Yo, we need you guys' help here," Guerrero explained to Diego and Kenny, while behind him the girls giggled and made shameless direct eye contact. "Gomez and I met these three lovely ladies who want to go to the movies. So we need a third male companion for . . ." He turned to the smallest of the female trio, who was peering from behind a curtain of permed hair. "What's your name?"

"Gaia," she squeaked.

"Your name's *Gaia*?" Gomez asked, cracking up. "That's so gay!"

The most brawny of the girls smacked her fist on Gomez's arm so hard that he stopped laughing.

"Look, either all three of us go," announced the third girl, "or none of us do." She was the tallest, a flaming redhead, and obviously the group leader.

"Come on, guys." Guerrero told Diego and Kenny. "One of you help us out here."

The girls were good-looking and seemed nice, but Diego wasn't interested. His heart was set on Ariel. He turned to Kenny, who often complained that girls treated him like he was irrelevant. "You go ahead."

But Kenny wasn't interested either. "Can't. I've got to go home." His tone was final, even though he told the girl, "Sorry."

Guerrero glowered at Kenny. "Yeah, we already know you're a mama's boy." Then he addressed Diego. "Come on, MacMann. I'll owe you one."

One what? Diego wondered. "I wish I could," he politely told the girls. "But I've got to go home too."

"Yo, come on!" Guerrero protested. "You and Kenny *both* got to go home? What are you, a couple?"

Diego took a breath, trying to keep calm. He could feel the anger rising inside him, from his gut through his chest, across his shoulders, and down into his curling fists, as he told Guerrero, "Shut up."

"Don't mind him," Kenny urged, tugging on Diego's arm. He seemed to sense Diego was about to lose his temper. "Let's go!"

"Yeah, never mind me," Guerrero chided. "Let's see you guys hold hands."

The girls behind him giggled, and Diego's head began to

burn. He leveled his gaze at Guerrero. "Screw you."

He'd almost said the stronger thing, but caught himself because of the girls, who now went silent, sucking their cheeks in worriedly. Guerrero bristled. And Kenny watched intently to see what would happen.

"*Screw me?*" Guerrero narrowed his eyes at Diego. "Instead of going to the movie with this good-looking babe you want to screw *me?*" Only he laughed at his joke. "You must really be a faggot."

In an instant, Diego sprang out at Guerrero, sending him reeling against the table and knocking over a chair. Unable to control himself, Diego leaped on top of him, pounding wildly with both fists. He punched and clobbered him without thinking, unaware of the girls screaming or Gomez trying to pull him off or Kenny shouting, "Stop it, Diego! Let him go! Stop!"

It took two mall security guards to pry him away and pin him down onto the food court floor. Next thing Diego knew, the police were handcuffing him while paramedics arrived to attend to Guerrero.

A woman police officer led Diego through a crowd and outside into a squad car, where she asked him a series of questions, writing his responses on a clipboard: Name. Age. Height. Weight.

"Have you ever been charged before?"

"Um, yeah," Diego admitted, figuring they'd find out anyway. "I'm on probation. Are you taking me to juvie?"

"You'd better believe it," the male officer said, starting the engine.

The car pulled out and the steel cuffs bit into Diego's wrists.
It's finally happening, he thought. To his surprise, he felt an odd sense of relief. At least he wouldn't have to wonder anymore if and when it might happen.

"Will you call my mom?" He could imagine how angry she'd be. Would she tell Eddie what had happened?

"They'll phone her from detention," the female officer replied.

Diego slumped down in the seat, wondering if Ariel would notice his absence at school. And what would Vidas say when he found out?

He stared out the window, remembering his last appointment and all the good things Vidas had pointed out about him. Obviously, the good wasn't enough to outweigh the bad. Even though he'd tried to deal with the anger, it was dealing with him—and winning.

CHAPTER 14

INSIDE THE JUVENILE DETENTION CENTER, the police released Diego from his handcuffs. In the process the intake officer spotted the cuts above his wrists.

"Remove your shirt," he told Diego, and although Diego didn't want to, he realized he didn't have much choice.

As Diego exposed the scars and slashes, the man let out a long, low whistle. "Boy, what did you do? Try to wrestle a propeller?"

Diego had to take off the shark's tooth and empty his pockets to make certain he didn't have any other sharp objects. The intake officer asked him questions about his health, school, family, and allergies. . . . Then he phoned Diego's mom, told her what had happened, and explained that she needed to go to court the next morning for Diego's detention hearing.

Diego listened anxiously, his heels bouncing on the carpet.

"She wants to talk to you," the man told him, holding out the receiver.

Diego inhaled a deep breath to brace himself, knowing how angry she'd be, and took the phone. "Um, hi."

"Is this what you want?" his mom demanded. "To throw your life away? Why should I even come tomorrow? I'm going to lose my job because of you."

Diego turned away from the intake officer, ducking his head in shame. What if his mom did lose her job because of him? What would happen to Eddie? Maybe they'd be better off to just leave him in juvie.

He covered the receiver's mouthpiece and whispered to the man, "Does she have to come tomorrow?"

"She'd better, or the judge will issue a summons."

Diego returned to the phone, listening until his mom stopped yelling and abruptly hung up. He couldn't blame her for being so angry.

The intake officer stared across the desk at him. "Are you okay?"

"Huh?" Diego replied. "Um, yeah."

The man shook his head. "I think we'd better put you on suicide watch."

"Why?" Diego asked, startled by the idea.

"With you showing up here like that"—he gestured to Diego's cuts—"I'm not taking any chances while you're under our custody."

Diego wasn't sure exactly what suicide watch meant until he was escorted to a cell separate from the other boys and told he had to strip down to his underwear.

"How come?" he protested.

"Those are the rules. Don't worry, you'll be by yourself.

In the morning you'll get your clothes back."

As Diego undressed, he glared at the man, feeling humili-
ated. It was a relief to step into the cell by himself. He didn't
feel locked in, but rather like everybody else was locked out.
He felt *safe* here—although he wasn't sure safe from what.

The white-walled concrete room, barely bigger than a
closet, was empty except for a vinyl mattress on the floor and
a gray blanket but no sheets. Against one wall were a metal
sink and a toilet without a seat. On the other wall was a barred
window to the outside. The place stank of disinfectant.

Diego plopped down onto the mattress, wrapped the
scratchy blanket around his shoulders, and recalled Vidas asking if he ever felt all alone. Right now he definitely did.

Occasionally, he heard the footsteps and muffled voices of
staff as they took turns making rounds, peering in the little
window of the thick steel door to make sure he wasn't offing
himself.

After a while he lay down and stared up at the encased fluo-
rescent lamp that glared brightly from the ceiling. There wasn't
any switch for it. He waited, wondering what time they'd turn
it off, until finally it occurred to him that they weren't going to;
they were leaving it on for suicide watch.

Unable to sleep with the glaring light, he stared at the
barred window, recalling when Vidas had told him he was
already in jail, a jail he was making for himself. Maybe this
was his destiny: to be locked in a real jail cell, where at least
he couldn't hurt anyone, not even himself.

He rolled over on the mattress, pulled the blanket over his
head, and eventually fell asleep. In the middle of the night, he

woke to the sound of someone crying. He drowsily listened,
wondering who the sound had come from. A boy in a neigh-
boring cell? Only as he drifted back to sleep, did he realize it was
the mattress beneath his own face that was damp with tears.

The next morning, a square-faced woman banged on the steel
door, rousing him, and tossed him a towel. "Time to go shower.
Come on, get a move on! This ain't summer camp."

The steam-filled shower room was packed with boys. Diego
braced himself for any possible confrontation and avoided eye
contact. Fortunately, the crowd ignored him, except for one
blond boy who shook his head at Diego's cuts and asked,
"What'd you get busted for?"

"A fight," Diego answered, and after that, nobody else said
anything to him.

During breakfast, most of the boys spoke at full volume,
clanged silverware, and clattered their trays. Diego kept to
himself until two bailiffs arrived to take him to court.

"You don't need those," he said as one pulled out handcuffs.

The officer ignored him and clamped the cuffs on anyway.

Unlike his previous court dates, this time he had to wait
in a holding cell—alone. The tiny room contained a concrete
bench and nothing else. His stomach turned when he noticed
that some of the prior inmates had left the only mark they
could on the cinder block walls: a crusty dried layer of green
and white spit.

A short while after he arrived, his mom appeared at the
door's Plexiglas window, her eyes concerned and her mouth
drooping in a frown.

"Are you okay?" she asked through the glass.

"Yeah. What did you tell Eddie?"

"That you're staying with a friend. If you care so much about him, why are you doing this?"

He shifted uncomfortably on the hard bench. "You think I want to be here?"

"Well, you're the one who put yourself here." They glowered at each other through the window, and then she walked away.

Several minutes later, the bailiff unlocked the door and let in Ms. Delgado. She wanted to know what had happened and Diego told her about the fight.

"So, now what'll happen to me?" he asked.

"The judge will set a trial date and decide whether to keep you in detention. I'll ask for your release . . ." She paused and gave him a wary look. ". . . unless you want to stay in jail."

"No!" Despite feeling safe in his dreary cell, he didn't want to go back. "Why would I want to stay there?"

"I don't know. Just don't pull any surprises like you did last time."

Diego glanced down at the scuffed tile floor, embarrassed. "I don't want to stay in jail."

"Okay," she replied. "I'll talk with Mr. Vidas. It may depend on what he recommends to the judge."

After Ms. Delgado left, Diego sat worried and waiting, till the bailiff suddenly unlocked the door again and let Vidas in.

"How're you feeling?" he asked as usual, looking directly into Diego's eyes.

Diego glanced away and said softly, "I messed up."

Vidas remained standing. Quiet. Waiting for Diego to say more.

"What else can I say?" Diego asked.

"Well," Vidas challenged him, "you'd better tell me more than that because this makes your second assault charge. The judge is going to want to know why you shouldn't stay locked up. Now, I can recommend that he let you go home till your trial, but you've got to give me something to work with."

Diego looked up. "What do you mean?"

"Start by telling me what happened," Vidas said and sat down on the bench beside him.

Diego took a deep breath before explaining about Guerrero. "He started to dis me. I didn't like it."

"What exactly did he say?" Vidas asked.

Diego glanced at him, but then looked down. "Stuff about me being gay."

"Isn't that what got you fighting last time?"

"I guess."

"I don't get it, Diego. You're smart. You know guys make jokes like that about everybody. So, what keeps triggering you to get so mad about it?"

Diego shook his head. "I just don't like them saying that about me."

Vidas was silent for a moment and rubbed his fingers across his brow. "Have you ever had thoughts about being with a guy?"

"No!" Diego pressed back against the wall.

"Maybe you've had dreams about it," Vidas persisted. "Boys

your age sometimes do. That doesn't mean you're gay. . . . But if you are, there's nothing shameful about it."

"I'm not gay!" Diego shot back. "I like *girls*. I think about Ariel all the time."

"All right." Vidas waited quietly, letting Diego's anger subside. "Then we're back at square one." He ran a hand across the back of his neck. "Think hard, Diego. Obviously, something happened that makes you so angry to be called gay. Only you can decide if you want to talk about it."

Diego looked straight at him and their eyes met. He felt more convinced than ever that Vidas somehow already knew what had happened.

Vidas brought his hand down from his neck. "I don't know what else to tell you, Diego. Like I said before, unless you open up, nobody can help you."

A war was raging in Diego. He wanted to slam open the door inside him and let out everything. But how could he admit what he'd let happen? If he hadn't wanted it to happen, why hadn't he stopped it?

"So, what will you tell the judge?" he asked.

"I'll tell him . . ." Vidas gave a brief sigh. ". . . that without you opening up, I've done all I can. Now it's up to him."

As Vidas stood to leave, Diego imagined being sent back to detention in handcuffs and locked into his depressing cell with its bare vinyl mattress, the stink of disinfectant, the bars on the window . . .

Vidas stepped toward the door to summon the bailiff. Diego gripped the edge of the concrete bench, and from deep within him came a whisper: "He touched me."

Vidas paused, inches from the door, and turned to Diego. "What?"

Diego's heart pounded as he looked Vidas squarely in the eye. Could he truly trust him? "Mac did stuff . . . to me."

Vidas lowered his hand and let out a long audible breath. "I understand."

"No, you don't!" Diego snapped. How could anybody understand the things Mac had made him do? "You *don't* understand!"

"All right," Vidas said and slowly eased back onto the bench. "Then help me to understand. Tell me about it."

Diego stared at him, glanced away, looked back. *Would* he understand? "What do you want to hear?"

"Whatever you want to tell me," Vidas said. "When did it start? Can you remember?"

"Yeah." He remembered as clear as if it happened last night. How could he *not* remember?

"When Mac began seeing my mom . . . and she left me at his hotel. While he and I watched TV, or swam in the pool, or wrestled on the floor his hands would sometimes . . . brush against me. You know?" Diego glanced an instant at his crotch. "At first I thought it was an accident, but it kept happening."

Diego paused, unable to believe he was telling another person this. Why wasn't Vidas freaking out, disgusted?

"I'm listening." Vidas leaned forward on the bench. "Go on."

"It felt weird," Diego continued. "Gross. But I didn't know what to say. I was only, like, six years old. I didn't even speak

English. And it wasn't like he was some skanky stranger. He brought my mom and me presents, took us places. Everybody said we were so lucky."

Diego took a breath, trying to slow down, but it was like opening a faucet. He'd kept so much bottled up for years.

"One time he took me on this fishing trip, overnight. I was so excited: my first boat trip. My mom couldn't go 'cause she gets seasick. We sailed out in the water till you couldn't see land—just ocean, everywhere—and he hooked this huge marlin that took hours to reel in. Then sharks started to appear. I was so scared. I'd never seen sharks in real life. And I thought, what if the boat sank?"

Diego swallowed hard, his throat as dry as if he'd swallowed seawater.

"The crew had to pull the marlin onto the deck to keep it from the sharks. They gutted it that night after dinner and threw the scraps over the side. The sharks went crazy fighting for them, climbing on top of one another, coming out of the water. I grabbed hold of Mac, terrified, shaking, and everybody laughed. They'd all been drinking. . . . Then he brought out his gun and fired at a shark. The shot was so loud. It was the first time I'd been around a real gun. You could feel the blowback. The shark twitched and spiraled away, then he shot another one. And I had this feeling, like something really bad is going to happen."

Diego hesitated, uncertain whether to keep going. But he couldn't stop.

"Between the sharks and the gun, I just wanted to get away.

So I went down to our cabin and crawled into bed, crying. I
remember holding my shark's tooth like that would protect
me, and fell asleep. Then, next thing I knew, he was climbing
into bed with me."

"Mac?" Vidas asked.

Diego nodded, amazed to be telling Vidas all this. He
never imagined he'd tell anybody.

"I could smell the whiskey on his breath, the cigarettes on
his skin. He circled his arms around me and I thought: *Just lay
still. He'll fall asleep and leave me alone.* But his hands started to
move all over me, sliding his fingers into my shirt and pushing
down my shorts."

Diego paused, remembering Mac kissing him. Not on the
cheek, like in front of his mom, but forcing his tongue into his
mouth. . . . The taste of alcohol and tobacco.

"I tried to push him off and get away but he was, like, twice
my size. 'No!' I told him. But he wouldn't let me go."

In his mind, Diego recalled Mac pressing against him. . . .
Shorts off. Grabbing Diego's hand, forcing it to touch him. He
couldn't tell Vidas that.

"I tried to get away, but my legs were tangled in my underwear, caught around my ankles. And I thought, *If I grab my
shark's tooth, I can cut him.* But he had my arms pinned."

Diego's voice became expressionless, like he was telling
someone else's story. And yet his heart raced as he recalled
Mac pressing into him from behind. And the pain. Excruciating
pain. Skin tearing, Mac pushing inside him.

"I cried for him to stop. But he covered my mouth and told

me he loved me, that I was his boy. My head was turned sideways and I saw his gun beside the bed and thought, *I'll get the gun.* But what if he used the gun on me? I was having all these mixed-up thoughts. And then . . ."

Diego hesitated, unsure about the next part.

"And then it was like . . . I was floating up into the air, looking down at my body. I could see what he was doing to me, except I wasn't inside my body anymore."

Diego paused, waiting for Vidas's reaction. "Do you think I'm crazy?"

"No." Vidas shook his head. "Other people describe leaving their bodies when raped."

Diego flinched. Why had Vidas said "raped"? Rape was something that happened to women, not guys.

"It's a way of dealing with the trauma," Vidas went on. "What else can you remember?"

It took Diego a moment to get back into the memory. "It was like I floated outside, over the ocean. It was night and so quiet. And there was this one shark, still circling the boat. . . . It rolled onto its side . . . and its eye looked up at me, like blaming me."

Diego had forgotten about that shark till now, just as he'd tried to forget about that night.

"Blaming you for what?" Vidas asked.

"I don't know. . . . For not stopping Mac maybe?"

Vidas nodded as though to register the answer. "What happened after that?"

"I guess I came back somehow. The next morning Mac put

his finger to his lips like what had happened was our secret,
and he didn't say anything about it. As if it never happened.
I remember thinking, *Well, maybe this is what dads do with their
sons.* I was so stupid! I wanted a dad so bad. I slept the whole
trip back; I hurt so much. At the pier, everybody was excited
about the trophy fish he'd caught."

"Did you tell your mom what happened?"

"I didn't know what to say." Diego slumped back against
the holding cell wall. "She saw my underwear stained and asked
what I'd eaten, as though I'd eaten something that made me
bleed. So I told her, 'No! Mac hurt me.' She gave me this blank
look. Then she raised her hand and slapped me, telling me not
to ever say anything like that again. She'd never hit me before.
Never. I started crying, sobbing. Then she cried too, putting
her arms around me, and said, 'He's going to marry me and
be your father and take us out of here. Do you understand?' It
was the only time she ever hit me. And after that I never told
anybody what happened."

Diego let out a long breath, exhausted and relieved, feeling like some weary swimmer finally reaching shore.

"That's a huge secret for a boy to carry," Vidas said, his eyes
brimming with compassion. "It took a lot of courage to trust
me with it."

Diego nodded, not quite believing he'd finally let the
secret out. He did trust Vidas—lots.

"I'm sorry it happened," Vidas continued. "You're not to
blame. You didn't deserve it."

"I know," Diego said, his lip beginning to tremble.

"You didn't deserve it," Vidas reiterated, as though to make sure Diego heard him.

Diego pulled his arms close next to him, feeling on the verge of tears.

A knock banged at the door and the bailiff spoke through the Plexiglas: "Ready? Your case is next."

A wave of apprehension seized Diego. He turned to Vidas. "You're not going to tell the judge all this, are you?

"Only if you want me to."

Diego shook his head and quickly wiped his cheeks. "No!"

"Then I won't." Vidas stood. "What the judge will want to know is: Are you going to keep assaulting people?"

Diego got shakily to his feet. "I don't want to." He knew it was a lame response, but it was the most honest one.

The bailiff unlocked the door and took a firm hold of Diego's arm, leading him to the courtroom, together with Vidas.

As Diego entered the courtroom, his mom turned to him from the front row, her face pained with worry. Diego glanced away, ashamed for her to see him like this, being led like a criminal. The bailiff released him at the defense table, where he slunk down into the chair beside Ms. Delgado and glanced up at the judge.

"So, what do we have here?" Judge Ferrara asked no one in particular and read aloud from a folder. "'Detention hearing for assault and battery.'" He adjusted his glasses and glanced at Diego, his eyes blinking with recognition. "Oh, I remember you. You're the smart aleck who told the court you should be on probation. Am I right?"

Diego's face flared red. Too embarrassed to answer, he glanced down at the table. From across the courtroom, Vidas replied for him: "Yes, your honor."

"Let the boy speak for himself," the judge grumbled, "since he's so smart."

Diego gazed up and tried to keep his voice steady. "Um, yes, your honor."

"Well, apparently"—Judge Ferrara's voice grew louder—"probation isn't enough for you. What do you think you need this time? To stay in jail?"

Diego swallowed the fist-size knot in his throat. "I don't know, sir."

"Oh, so you're not so smart anymore!" the judge said and turned to the prosecutor. "What does the county recommend?"

"As you'll note, your honor"—the prosecutor stood to speak—"this is Mr. MacMann's second assault. He clearly presents a danger to the community. For that reason, we request detention till trial."

Diego listened in disbelief. *A danger to the community?*

"Counsel, what's your response?" Judge Ferrara asked Ms. Delgado.

"Your honor"—she got up from her chair—"while we appreciate this is a serious charge, I'd like to point out that overall Diego is doing well. He makes good grades. He behaves at home. And Mr. Vidas reports that except for this incident, Diego has abided by the terms of probation, including restitution—which he paid out of savings from his weekend job. I believe that given these factors, keeping him out of his home, work, and school would do more harm than good."

She sat down again and the judge leaned back in his leather chair. His somber gaze moved to Diego's mom. "He behaves well at home?"

"Yes, your honor." Her voice came out shaky and uneven.

"He's a good boy. He helps me a lot with his little brother."

"His little brother?" Judge Ferrara scoffed. "You think he's setting a good example?"

Diego withered in his seat as his mom replied, "No, not with this, your honor."

The judge shifted his gaze across the room. "What light can you shed on this, Mr. Vidas?"

Diego's legs began to jiggle beneath the table. Would Vidas keep his word not to say anything about what he'd told him?

"Your honor," Vidas began, "as Diego's counsel stated, overall he's responded well to probation. Apart from this incident, he's made progress in dealing with what I believe is the core of his anger. Unfortunately, as you're aware, sometimes it's two steps forward and one step back."

Diego relaxed a fraction. Obviously Vidas was on his side. But Judge Ferrara scowled, unpersuaded. "And a step back means he assaults someone again?"

Vidas pressed his lips together without answering.

The judge refocused his glare on Diego. "So, Mr. Smart Aleck! I'm not convinced that you won't go off on somebody else. Maybe with three more days of detention it might sink in: If you keep this up, your new home will be jail." He jabbed his thick finger at Diego. "*Comprende?*"

Diego nodded, picturing his bleak cell. "Yes, your honor."

Outside the courtroom, he was allowed only a few seconds to visit with his mom. He expected her to scold him again but instead she wrapped her arms around him, her eyes shiny with tears.

"Take care of yourself," she told him. *"¡Cuídate!"*

A second bailiff handcuffed him again to return him to juvie.

Seeing his mom so upset unsettled Diego, making him feel like he'd betrayed her. What if Vidas told her what Diego revealed and blamed her for not stopping Mac? Would she get in trouble? Without her, what would happen to Eddie—and to him?

As soon as he got back to the detention center, he asked the intake officer, "Can you phone my PO? I need to talk to him."

"We'll put in a call," the man replied. "Now go eat lunch."

Diego was picking at a plate of ham and mashed potatoes, feeling too tense to eat, when the loudspeaker blared across the dining hall: "Diego MacMann! Your PO's on the phone."

Diego hurried to the office, pressed the phone to his ear, and blurted into the receiver, "Is my mom going to get in trouble?"

"Your mom?" Vidas asked, confused. "Get in trouble for what?"

"Because of—you know—the stuff I told you."

The other end of the line was silent a moment. "Diego, I'm trying to help you and your family, not hurt you. Don't you understand that?" Vidas paused and waited for him to say something, but Diego didn't know what to say.

"Tell you what," Vidas continued. "I'll make a deal with you. I won't tell anybody about what you told me unless I check with you first. In turn, you stay out of trouble in detention and we'll talk more at your next appointment. Deal?"

The reassurance helped to calm Diego a little. The remainder of the day, he kept to himself, ignoring the other boys as they called each other "fag" and "homo." Vidas was right: Guys teased each other that way all the time. He'd been stupid to let it get to him.

When bedtime arrived, he learned that he was still under suicide watch. Once again, he had to strip to his underwear, and the steel door locked behind him. He dropped onto the bare mattress, the stink of disinfectant wafting up at him.

In the silence of the cell, the fresh memory of Mac and the boat began to flash back through his mind. With each image, his heartbeat quickened, his chest tightened. When the staff came around, it was Mac's face that peered through the door window, once again coming to get him, wanting him.

Diego scrambled back against the concrete wall. His breath came deep and fast. Even though the face disappeared, he felt like he couldn't get enough air. His fingers gouged into his skin, wanting to peel the flesh off. Anything to make his feelings go away. Desperate, he slammed his fist against the cell block wall. A surge of pain shot up his arm. A sudden liquid heat filled his body. And his panic slowly subsided.

He lay back down, cradling his aching arm beneath the rough blanket. He hated this place. He hated his life. He hated himself.

The next three days dragged on forever. Meals consisted of mountainous heaps of food, as if to keep the kids busy eating.

After breakfast, all detainees were supposed to do schoolwork, but instead most horsed around—clowning, punching, burping, farting, climbing out of their seats, yelling over at the girls, throwing paper, calling each other "queer," making noise, noise, and more noise—while the staff kept shouting at them to do their work.

Diego reminded himself of his deal with Vidas and stayed out of trouble. He was one of a handful of inmates who actually did any schoolwork, and the staff asked him to help this quiet Mexican boy his same age who could barely read any better than eight-year-old Eddie. It reminded Diego of how much he missed his brother.

The other person he thought a lot about was Ariel—especially at night, when he lay alone in his cell. He stared up at the metal-barred window to the outside, recalling their kiss and wondered, would she even talk to him anymore after this?

During the afternoons, while the girls stayed in a separate area, the boys were set loose onto a basketball court. Diego sat at the edge of the concrete, leaning against the thirteen-foot-high barbwire-topped fence, and watched them play, push, and knock into one another while he waited for the time to pass.

Following dinner, everybody had to stay in a central area, where they watched the blaring TV, argued over programs, played cards, and made up rap lyrics. Again, the noise was earsplitting.

During his last evening, Diego found an old tattered scuba diving magazine. He'd always wanted to learn to skin-dive but that cost money, more than he'd ever had. After flipping through the magazine photos, he read an article about a diver who'd actually faced off a shark—and had survived.

Perhaps the story led to the unsettling dream Diego had that night. It began on an ocean beach with Vidas. In his hand, Vidas held an orange-colored starfish and was playing a version of hide-and-seek. While Diego closed his eyes, Vidas would bury the starfish in the sand. Then, Diego had to hunt for it and dig it up. When he brought the starfish back, Vidas threw it into the surf and told him, "Now try to find it!"

Diego waded into the waves and searched through the water but couldn't see the starfish anywhere. Vidas told him, "Maybe you should ask your shark to help you."

With that, the dream changed to the middle of the open ocean, where Diego floated under the surface in a metal-barred cage like in shark-diving videos. Even though he didn't have scuba gear, he was somehow breathing underwater. And circling him was the ghostly form of the shark.

Above him on a boat, Vidas was throwing scraps into the water for the shark. And the food was falling into Diego's cage.

"Stop!" Diego shouted underwater, bubbles streaming out of his mouth. "Stop it!"

Unable to hear him, Vidas kept tossing scraps. The shark moved closer to the cage, baring its huge teeth. Suddenly it charged. The massive jaws rammed through the steel bars.

Diego woke up screaming and slammed against the cell wall. His skin shone wet with sweat in the light from overhead. Catching his breath, he stared up at the metal bars of the window and thought about the dream. It made no sense.

Why had Vidas fed the shark and let the scraps get into Diego's cage? Was he trying to hurt Diego?

Too disturbed by the nightmare to fall back asleep, Diego stayed awake, waiting for morning and the staff to let him out.

CHAPTER 16

ON THE MORNING of Diego's release from detention, he got back the shark's tooth and replaced it around his neck while waiting for his mom. From the moment she drove up, he noticed the cross look in her eyes.

"I can't miss any more work," she scolded him on the drive to school. "Next time you get locked up, you can stay there."

He glared across the car at her. Why did she always have to undermine him? She never believed in him. "There won't be a next time," he muttered. "How's Eddie?"

"Crazy to see you. Don't tell him about jail, okay? He doesn't know."

Once again she was making him keep secrets, but he couldn't really blame her. He didn't want Eddie to know he'd been in jail either.

"Has Mr. Vidas phoned you?" Diego asked, anxious to find out if he'd kept his secret.

"No," his mom replied. "Why? Was he supposed to?"

"No. Just wondering."

They were both quiet until his mom's expression softened. "Ariel called."

"She did?" Diego sat up. "You didn't tell her, did you?"

"I didn't have to. She'd already heard about it."

Diego slumped back in his seat. Would Ariel want any more to do with him?

"You look like you put on weight," his mom said. "Was the food good?"

"It was all right," Diego mumbled, his mind still on Ariel.

At school, he was required to meet with the vice principal for discipline before he could be admitted.

"Let's get one thing clear"—Mr. Wesson leaned across his desk toward Diego—"I don't care how good your grades are, I won't tolerate criminals in my school."

"I'm not a criminal," Diego protested.

"Then stop acting like one. If you give even a hint of trouble, I'm tossing you out of here. Got that?"

Diego felt like walking out right then and there. Just forget school. But instead he muttered, "Got it."

When he walked to class, it seemed as though people stared at him and steered clear. Maybe he was just being paranoid.

As he approached his locker, he saw Guerrero for the first time since the mall. Gauze covered his nose, apparently broken during their scuffle. Seeing him bandaged up like that gave Diego a twinge of guilt, but not enough to apologize. At least now Guerrero kept his mouth shut and left him alone.

At the sight of Diego, Kenny burst into a huge smile. During lunch he asked, "So how was juvie?"

"It stank. Literally." He'd missed Kenny, the friend he knew he could always count on, no matter what. "You want to come over after school?"

"Sure." Kenny nodded eagerly. "You bet."

At the end of the day, Diego spotted the other person he wanted to see. She was standing across the hall at her locker. Upon seeing him, her expression tightened. The friends she was with exchanged glances and leaned close to her—probably telling her that he was beyond sketchy; he was bad news.

He closed his locker, said a prayer, and walked toward her. She flashed a glance at her friends and they moved a few lockers away, their cold stares fixed on him.

"Um, hi," he said, not knowing what else to say.

"Hi." Although her voice had an edge, she didn't sound angry. "Are you okay?" she asked.

"Yeah, thanks." He jammed his hands into his pockets. "Um, how are you?"

"I'm very upset." Her eyes abruptly clouded. "I was worried about you. I don't get why you keep hurting people."

His skin grew hot beneath her gaze. He wanted to tell her the fight wasn't his fault, that Guerrero had started it. But instead he hung his head, ashamed for disappointing her.

"If you, um, don't want to see me anymore, I won't blame you. If I were you, I wouldn't want to—"

"Diego!" She sounded even more upset than before. "You don't get it, do you? I *care* about you."

Diego leaned back on his heels, startled by her response. How could she care about him? Wasn't it obvious how messed-up he was?

"Don't say that unless you mean it," he told her.

"If I didn't mean it," she countered, "why would I say it?"

He glanced down at the floor tile. "But you don't know me."

"I'm trying to," she replied. "Are you going to let me?"

He wanted to let her, but . . . "What do you want me to say?"

"To start, you can explain why you're always getting into fights."

Diego flashed back to Vidas telling the judge about getting to the core of Diego's anger: the Mac stuff. How could he ever let her know about that?

Instead he explained, "Guerrero started messing with me. I lost my temper."

"So will the same thing happen," she challenged, "if you lose your temper with me?"

"No!" How could she compare herself with Guerrero? "I would never hurt you. Never."

"You already have," she told him, her voice pained. "When you hurt somebody like you did, you hurt yourself, too, and it hurts me to hear about it. I want to care about you, Diego. But only if you decide you're going to care about yourself."

She stared at him so hard that he had to avert his eyes.

"Give me a call when you make up your mind," she told him. And with that, she turned and walked away, rejoining her friends.

He shuffled back to his locker and found Kenny waiting.

"I think I just screwed up again."

Kenny pressed his glasses up the bridge of his nose. "Did she dump you?"

"Um, no. I don't think so."

"Did you dump her?" Kenny asked.

"No."

"Then what's the screw-up?"

Diego shrugged with frustration. "I just don't know if I can do this dating thing."

"Well, if you're not dumping each other, I think you're already doing it."

Diego pondered that as they rode the bus to his house, where Kenny helped him catch up on the classwork he'd missed while in juvie.

Later that evening, as Diego made dinner, Eddie asked, "Why did you stay at your friend's house so many days?"

Diego hesitated. Should he tell him the truth about jail, even though he'd promised not to? He didn't want to lie; he wanted to be a good example. But he also didn't want Eddie to know what a mess-up he was.

He put his arm around his little brother's shoulder and told him, "Look, I made a mistake. I'm sorry. I won't do it again. Okay?"

Even though he wasn't being fully honest, it was the best he could do.

CHAPTER 17

ON SATURDAY MORNING, Diego biked to work without eating breakfast, his stomach too knotted up with worry. Would he get fired for having been in jail?

His boss, Mrs. Patel, greeted him as usual, with a list of chores. Hadn't she heard about his arrest? Despite feeling guilty about it, he decided not to bring it up. Instead, he worked extra hard all day and stopped only for a quick pizza slice. When his shift ended at six, he asked, "Um, is there anything else I can do?"

"You're a hard worker," Mrs. Patel replied with a knowing look. "Learn to cool that fire in your belly and you'll do okay in life."

Diego swallowed hard. Was she hinting that she'd heard about his arrest? He held his breath, waiting for her next words.

"See you next Saturday," she said.

"Thanks," he told her, and raced his bike straight home, determined to stay out of any more trouble.

The following week, he arrived at his probation appointment early—still apprehensive about the things he'd admitted to Vidas but eager to talk about Ariel.

"How're you feeling?" Vidas asked as Diego sank into his usual green vinyl chair.

"Good," Diego replied, taking a candy from the jar Vidas extended to him. He liked being back in the familiar office. "Um, can I talk to you about something?"

"Anything," Vidas replied, unwrapping his own candy. "I'm listening."

"Well, it has to do with—you know—the girl I went on a date with?"

"You mean Ariel?" Vidas asked.

"Yeah!" It amazed him that Vidas remembered her name.

"How's it going with her?"

"Well, um, I thought she'd be mad at me for getting locked up but instead . . ." Diego felt himself grow warm inside his shirt. "She said she cares about me. I think something's wrong with her."

"Because she cares about you?"

"Right." Diego cracked his knuckles nervously.

"Diego, everybody has good points and bad. Clearly, she sees your good points."

"Yeah, but she doesn't know how *many* bad points I have. What if she finds out and dumps me?"

"That's the risk we take," Vidas said, "whenever we open up

to someone. What are the bad points you're worried about?"

"*You* know," Diego said, but Vidas gave no acknowledgment.

"The stuff I told you," Diego explained impatiently. "About Mac."

"How have you felt about that," Vidas asked, "since you told me?"

Diego slid his hands beneath his thighs. He wanted to talk about Ariel, not Mac. "I haven't felt anything."

"You must feel something," Vidas insisted. "That was a pretty major secret to tell me." He pointed to the smiley-face poster. "Pick a feeling."

Diego scanned the faces. His gaze landed on a squiggle mouth with a pair of eyebrows pointed upward. "Embarrassed, I guess."

"Embarrassed?" Vidas's brow crinkled. "You've got nothing to feel embarrassed about, Diego. You did nothing wrong. He abused you."

Diego's legs began to jiggle. He wished Vidas would stop using words like "rape" and "abuse."

"I should've stopped him."

"How?" Vidas asked. "You were a little boy. He was a grown man."

Diego glanced down at the floor. "I could've fought him harder."

"Diego . . ." Vidas spoke slowly, measuring each phrase. "You wanted a dad. . . . You wanted to be loved. . . . There's no shame in that. . . . You trusted him. He violated that trust. . . . You didn't do anything wrong. *He* did."

Diego listened carefully, absorbing every word. And yet he still felt at fault.

"After that night on the boat," Vidas said gently. "It happened again, didn't it?"

Diego looked up from the carpet, wondering how Vidas knew.

"Want to tell me about it?" Vidas asked.

"What for?" Diego balked. "It won't change anything."

"It might. Talking out your secrets can help *you* change."

Diego gazed out the window at the boats in the harbor and recalled the dream he'd had his last night in detention: Him in the ocean and Vidas feeding the shark.

"It didn't happen again for a long time," Diego admitted. "Not like on the boat. When Mac came to visit us, he acted like that night had never happened. And so did I. Sometimes I thought maybe it hadn't really happened. Maybe I'd just dreamed it."

Diego paused, wishing it truly had been only a dream.

"He brought us presents and clothes, like if Santa had arrived. All our neighbors were jealous. Everybody liked him."

"That must've been confusing," Vidas interjected.

"Yeah." Diego nodded. "While Ma worked, she'd leave me at his hotel. We watched TV and he'd start to drink. His face would get this look: needylike . . . and then he'd put his hands on me. . . . I hated it. I wanted him to stop. But then I remembered Ma slapping me and telling me I shouldn't say anything."

Diego watched Vidas carefully, worried again that he'd get his mom in trouble. But Vidas showed no interest in pursuing details about his mom.

"So I thought," Diego continued, "if I just let him do that, at least he won't do the other thing, like on the boat. I just watched TV till he finished. Afterward he'd tell me how much he loved me, acting like some kid who'd been given a present. I'd block out what happened, telling myself it hadn't been that bad. After all, I had friends whose dads beat them, whose parents yelled at them and said horrible things. At least Mac didn't do that. He never hit me."

"But what he did to you *was* horrible," Vidas countered. "Just as bad, if not worse. You didn't deserve that, Diego."

Diego's legs jiggled faster. "So then my mom married him, he adopted me, and we moved here."

"That was a big change," Vidas observed. "How'd you feel about it?"

"Excited. I wanted to see snow. Everybody had always said how great the U.S. was. We moved into a huge apartment compared to our one tiny little room in Mexico. Ma said this would be a new start for us."

"Was it?" Vidas asked. "Or did Mac continue to molest you?"

Diego flinched at the word "molest." A molester was some perv who hid behind bushes, not his own stepdad.

"Sometimes," Diego replied. "When he took me somewhere in the car, he'd stop and park. . . . You know? And afterward he'd take me for ice cream, just like normal;

never talk about what he'd just done. I wanted to run away,
tell somebody. But who? And what if they sent us back to
Mexico?"

Diego brought his hand to his forehead and rubbed a
circle. What would've happened to Mac if Diego had told
somebody? Would he still have killed himself? Or might he
still be alive? A sudden rash of guilt prickled Diego's skin. It
was too overwhelming to think about all that.

"So then Eddie was born and Ma put the crib in their room.
But he cried a lot. One night when he kept crying, Mac came
to sleep with me. That's when it happened again, like on the
boat."

He could recall the doorknob's click, footsteps across his
carpet, bedcovers pulled back, and Mac's body, warm and
huge. . . . His hand, smelling of cigarettes, covering Diego's
mouth . . . The feeling like he couldn't breathe, like he wanted
to throw up . . . And the pain, so great it made him cry.

"Diego . . . ?" Vidas called softly.

"Huh?" He realized he'd zoned out.

"You need some water?" Vidas asked, pouring a cup from
the plastic bottle on his desk.

Diego downed the water in almost a single gulp.
"Thanks."

"What were you remembering?" Vidas said.

"Um, wanting to throw up." Diego pitched the empty cup
into the trash can. "Maybe if I had, it would've stopped him."

Vidas stared silently. "You're blaming yourself again. It
wasn't your fault."

Diego knew that—in his head. But he didn't feel it.

"Did your mom ever question why he didn't just sleep on the couch?"

"That's what *I* asked her. But she told me his back hurt and I was being ungrateful after all he'd done for us."

"Did *you* think you were ungrateful?"

"I didn't know what to think. In the morning he drove me to school and gave me lunch money, telling me he loved me. And at night he watched TV and played games with Eddie and me, like everything was normal. Even after Eddie got older and stopped crying at night, whenever Mac and Ma fought, he'd come to my room."

"How'd it feel," Vidas asked, "to live a secret life like that?"

"I stopped feeling anything," Diego said, his voice flat. "What was the point? I thought, *He'll never let you go. No matter how hard you try. There's nothing you can do. So, just stop feeling.*"

"And now?" Vidas said. "How do you feel?"

"I just want to cut out the whole memory."

Vidas gazed down at Diego's arms. "You mean like with that shark's tooth?"

Diego didn't get what Vidas was saying at first; then he understood. "I guess so."

Vidas nodded and Diego continued: "Sometimes I have this huge sense, like this isn't who I'm supposed to be, this isn't the life I was supposed to have, this wasn't supposed to happen. But there's nothing I can do about it. . . . It's too late now. . . . May as well just end it."

Vidas leaned forward slightly in his swivel chair. "End what?"

"End *me*," Diego said. His voice was emotionless. "I read once about this thing called 'the call of the waters,' where sometimes a sailor pitches himself off his ship into the ocean. Nobody knows why. . . . But *I* do. It's like there's something pulling at me, some undertow that's caught me, and no matter how hard I fight it, I'm going under. I'm a goner. May as well just give it up, you know?"

"No." Vidas shook his head emphatically. "You're not a goner. You've got a lot to live for. It takes courage to face the things you're telling me. You're probably the bravest boy on my caseload. You can get through this. Just don't give up. Okay? Never give up."

Diego curled both fists beneath his chin and rested his head on them, listening. No one had ever called him brave before. And yet even now he could feel the dark current pulling at him, wanting him to die.

"I'm concerned about you," Vidas said, looking directly into his eyes. "Is it only a feeling you've had? Or have you thought about how you'd do it?"

Is there a difference? Diego wondered. "I used to think about using his gun."

"Where's the gun now?" Vidas asked.

"The police took it."

Vidas relaxed a little and Diego continued, "Now I'm not sure how I'd do it—probably just swim out into the ocean till the sharks ate me . . . or I just couldn't swim anymore . . . the call of the waters . . ."

Vidas tapped his fingers on the chair arm, clearly worried. "Do you still have my card?"

"Yeah."

"Good. Can I see it?"

Diego pulled the card from his wallet and handed it to him.

Vidas grabbed a pen. "I'm going to write down the number of the suicide hotline. If you—"

"I'm not calling that," Diego interrupted, "and talking to some stranger."

Vidas ignored his protest, wrote the number down, and handed the card back. "You can also leave me a message at my number here. Anytime, day or night. Even if you just start to think about suicide, I want you to promise you'll call me. Can you agree to that?"

Diego nodded, though he wasn't sure he meant it.

"I care about you, Diego."

Diego squirmed in his chair, feeling hugely uneasy. It was hard enough to hear "I care about you" from Ariel; it made him ten times more nervous to hear it from a guy.

"How're you feeling now?" Vidas asked.

"Good," Diego lied, tired and wanting to leave.

"You sure?" Vidas pressed. "Anything else you want to talk about?"

"Nope."

"All right," Vidas said. "You might have some strong feelings come up after today. Call me if you need to talk, okay?"

He walked Diego down the hall as usual, telling him, "Bike safely!"

As Diego rode toward home along the seawall, he watched the tide receding down across the rocks, exposing the seaweed and barnacles. At moments it felt almost as if the current was reaching up and pulling him, too. And he wasn't sure he had the strength to fight it.

CHAPTER 18

ON FRIDAY NIGHT, after making macaroni and cheese for dinner, Diego found himself staring at the phone, longing to talk with Ariel. He'd replayed their kiss at least fourteen thousand times in his mind. And yet he hesitated to call. Eventually, she was bound to find out just how messed-up he was, and never go out with him again. So, why bother?

If only he'd talked to Vidas more about her—and less about Mac. Vidas made him feel like he stood a chance with her. What would Vidas tell him now? After considering for a moment, Diego carried the phone into his room and closed the door.

"Um, hi," he mumbled when she answered. "It's me, Diego."

"I know," she said softly. "I've been hoping you'd call."

"Really?"

"Yeah," replied Ariel. "I'd begun to think maybe you weren't interested anymore."

"I'm interested." He sat himself on the bed to keep his legs from shaking. "I just thought—you know—maybe you didn't really want me to call."

"Why wouldn't I want you to call?"

"Well . . ." He wrapped a finger through a belt loop of his jeans. "Because of all my problems . . . getting into fights, being locked up . . ."

Ariel was quiet a moment before answering. "Diego, we've all got problems. Everybody does."

"Not like mine," he insisted.

"Well, then, you're special," Ariel said, as if trying to end the topic. Was she being sarcastic? Or did she really think he was special? Before he could ask, she announced, "My mom found out you were in juvie."

"She did?" He hadn't expected that. "What did she say? Is she mad?"

"Not exactly mad . . . More like worried. She said I should find somebody else to date."

He bit into his lip, certain she was about to dump him.

"But I told her," Ariel continued, "I don't want to date anybody else."

He sat up straighter. "You told her that?"

"Yeah."

"Why?" Why was she so bent on dating him?

"Because," she explained, "I think your tough-guy act is just a front. I don't believe you're really that person. It doesn't match the shy guy who's always so nervous to talk to me."

Diego listened and wondered, where was she going with this?

"Anyway," she continued, "Mom says that she knows she

can't stop me from seeing you and that if I'm determined, she wants to talk to you."

Little beads of sweat exploded onto Diego's forehead. "You mean right *now*?"

"No, not now. She wants you to come for lunch on Sunday after church. Can you make that?"

"Um, sure." He wiped his brow with a sleeve, more worried than ever. What would her mom say to him?

Ariel switched topics after that, wanting to know what juvie had been like and asking about his mom's reaction. He was relieved when the conversation finally turned to homework, school, and recent TV.

After hanging up, he lay back in bed, staring at the ceiling, mystified that she was still interested in him. Was there a chance they might become a couple at some point? Or, like Kenny had implied, were they already one? That possibility made him jump up from bed to high-five the ceiling, feeling like he could almost touch the sky.

For the next thirty-six hours, nearly the only thing he could think about was his upcoming date. On Saturday during his lunch break, he walked to the drugstore to buy a new bag of gummies for Ariel. While in the checkout line, he noticed a box of chocolates. Maybe he should get them for her mom. It could only help.

On Sunday afternoon he biked to Ariel's, pulled the gifts from his backpack, and rang the doorbell.

From inside came excited barking, and a moment later Ariel answered the door, her dogs beside her.

"Thanks," she told Diego as he handed her the gummy bears. "You're going to spoil me."

"And these are for your mom." He held out the chocolate box.

"Cool. But *you* should give them to her. She won't bite, you know."

Inside the house, a good smell of tomato sauce, sautéed onions, and peppers came from the kitchen, where Ariel's mom was pulling a tray of lasagna from the oven.

"Um, hi," Diego told her, and Ariel announced, "He brought you something."

Her mom set the lasagna on the counter. When she pulled off her oven mitts, Diego handed her the chocolates.

"Oh, that's sweet." Her mom gave him a look as if to say, *I guess you can't be all bad.*

He helped Ariel to set the table and pour beverages, trying not to spill anything. During lunch, he felt so nervous he could barely swallow.

"I understand," Ariel's mom said, "that you were arrested and put in detention for getting into a fight?"

His face turned hot as an oven. "Um, yes, ma'am."

"So," she continued, "are you going to learn to control your temper?"

"I want to, ma'am. I'm trying."

Her skeptical stare made him wither. He glanced at Ariel, hoping to draw some encouragement, and she looked back hopefully.

"Well, let me be clear," her mom said. "If you ever hurt my

daughter, lift a hand against her at all, I will personally see to it that you get put away for a very, very long time."

"Mom!" Ariel exclaimed. "You're being hysterical."

"No, I'm not." Her mom kept her gaze on Diego. "Am I being clear?"

"Yes, ma'am," he replied, wishing he could evaporate.

After they'd finished eating, he helped Ariel to clear the table and accidentally dropped a glass, cracking it, he was so jittery. *Oh, great,* he thought and mumbled, "Sorry."

"Don't worry about it," she whispered, and buried the glass in the bottom of the trash so her mom wouldn't see it.

They loaded the dishwasher without any more mishaps and she told her mom they were going to watch a DVD. When they got to the den, he relaxed a little. They picked out a movie and while Ariel loaded it, he checked on her aquarium.

"Your tank looks clear and healthy," he observed. "You've got room for more fish, if you want."

"What would you suggest?" She walked over and stood beside him.

"Well, your tetras and harlequins are mid-layer fish. See how they hover near the middle?"

"I'd noticed that." She bent over to look and he glanced down at her hair, imagining the feel of it brushing his cheek.

"Yeah, so, um, you might consider adding a bottom fish. Personally, I like leopard corydoras. They're neat-looking and scavenge for fallen food."

"Wow, you know a lot."

"Sort of. For the top, near the surface, scissor tails are fun

to watch. You should come into the store one Saturday. I'll
help you."

"Okay." She grinned and led him to the sofa, sitting so close to him that he could smell the perfume on her skin—a clean citrus scent that he really liked.

As the movie started, she said in a gentle voice, "I'm sorry about my mom. She gets a little overprotective—"

"But she's right," Diego interrupted. "If I ever hurt you, I *should* be put in jail. I'd never forgive myself."

Ariel glanced into his eyes, studying him. "I think she's that way because of my dad. When I was in fifth grade, they started to get into arguments all the time. Then one day he hit her."

Diego leaned back, a little shocked, and she noticed his surprise.

"I warned you," she told him, "my life has been a little sketchy too. I wasn't there that first time. All I knew was they tried going to counseling. But one night he got drunk and hit her again. That time I saw it." Ariel's face tightened. "The police came. . . . I was so scared. After that, my mom made him move out. Then they got divorced. For two years I didn't want to see him."

No wonder her mom was concerned about her. Hearing her story made Diego want to wrap his arms around her, just hold her.

"Eventually he went to AA," Ariel continued, "and he stopped drinking. Now he has a new family and takes me to dinner once a week. So you see? My life's hardly been normal."

Diego drew a breath, trying to think of the right thing to

say. Then he recalled what Vidas had said to him in the hold-ing cell.

"I'm sorry that happened to you. You didn't deserve it."

"Thanks." She smiled a little sadly. "I just hope you don't run away."

"I won't," he assured her, and noticed her eyes were moist.

"Now it's your turn," she said. Pointing the remote, she turned off the DVD they'd been ignoring. "Tell me about you."

With the TV off, the room seemed painfully silent. His throat tightened. "Um, like, what do you want to know?"

"I want to know you, who you are." She took hold of his hand, slipping her fingers between his. "Like I told you about me."

"Well, um . . ." His legs jiggled uncontrollably. In spite of the things she'd told him about her dad, he wasn't ready to tell her about Mac. ". . . Like I said before, my life has been kind of complicated."

"Yeah . . . ?" she said encouragingly.

He gazed down at the carpet, wishing he could tell her more, but no matter how much he wanted to, the words just wouldn't come. Why couldn't she simply accept him without wanting to know so much? He felt her staring at him, waiting.

"What are you so afraid of?" she asked. "That I won't like you? Well, I'm afraid you won't like me, but I'm being honest with you."

He felt the sweat between their palms as a sea of emotions

swirled inside him. He wanted to be honest with her, too. But what could he say that wouldn't pull him in over his head? His free hand fidgeted with the sofa cushion. "It's, um, about my stepdad . . . stuff he did."

Her brow crinkled as she peered into his eyes. "You mean stuff he did *to you*?"

Diego's heart nearly zoomed out of his throat. How'd she figured that out? Had she guessed what he meant? Would she tell people at school? He'd never be able to show his face again. Why had he told her anything? He couldn't sit still a second longer.

"I've got to go." He pulled his hand away, standing up.

Everything became a blur after that: what she said, what her mom said, getting on his bike . . . Next thing he knew, he was racing down the street toward his house, breathing in huge gulps of air, panicked by even the little bit he'd told her. To make matters worse, he realized he'd left behind his backpack, but there was no way he'd go back for it.

CHAPTER 19

AFTER DIEGO ARRIVED HOME, Ariel phoned but he didn't want to talk with her, not after what he'd revealed, and running out like he had. The following morning, he slammed the alarm off and buried his head beneath the pillow, dreading facing her at school.

The third time his snooze went off, his mom came in and shook his shoulder. "Are you getting up or do I have to call Mr. Vidas?"

It was the first time she'd threatened to phone his PO. He blinked his eyes open, remembering that school was part of his contract. He had to go.

Since he'd left his backpack at Ariel's, he had to use an old satchel and barely made it to his bus in time. When he got to school, he skulked down the hallway, hoping to avoid her, but she appeared at his locker, holding his backpack.

"Um, thanks." He took the bag, barely looking her in the eye.

"Why'd you run out yesterday?" she asked.

He shifted his feet. "I just had to go . . . that's all."

"Are you okay?" she asked.

"Um, yeah. Fine. Fine."

"You don't seem fine."

"I am." He forced himself to glance at her for an instant but had to look away.

"All right," she said as the bell rang. "Call me whenever you want to talk."

Talk? What could he possibly say? He'd already revealed too much.

On Thursday after school, Diego biked to the courthouse, eager to talk with Vidas about what had happened. The receptionist greeted him with a surprised look.

"Didn't your school give you my message? Mr. Vidas got stuck in a trial—still going on. He's sorry he can't meet with you today but he'll see you next week."

Diego remained standing at the counter, debating what to do. He really wanted to talk to Vidas. "Um, can I wait for him?"

"You can if you want . . . but the trial could run all afternoon."

"I'll wait." Diego sat down beside the other boys in a row of chairs. As one boy after another met with a PO and then left, Diego stayed seated, watching the minutes tick by on the wall clock. Each time footsteps echoed in the tile hallway, he hoped it would be Vidas, but it wasn't.

At 5:20, Mrs. Ahern started to clean up behind her counter as other staff said bye on their way to the elevator. When the clock hands reached 5:30, she stood to leave.

"I'm afraid you'll need to go now," she told Diego. "You can't stay here by yourself. Mr. Vidas will see you next week. Or you can call him before that. Okay?"

Diego didn't want to talk on the phone; it wouldn't be the same as seeing him. It made him angry that Vidas had blown off their appointment, for whatever reason. If Diego had to keep his appointments, then why didn't Vidas?

After biking home, Diego made dinner for Eddie and him, then retreated to his room. Still angry, he pulled the shark's tooth out, peeled his shirt off, and examined the tangle of scars that snaked up his arms and across his chest.

He settled on an unmarked spot on his right bicep and pressed the tooth against his skin. A prick of pain pierced through him. And a tiny bead of blood hemorrhaged out. But this time there was no excitement, no thrill.

As he sliced the tooth across his flesh, his mind remained on Vidas. He knew that he'd tell him about this, and Vidas would listen understandingly. Now that the cutting was no longer a secret, it seemed kind of stupid. What was the point? Rather than take his feelings away, it was only making him madder. He pulled the tooth away from his skin and grabbed a tissue, staunching the blood flow, and thought how Vidas was making his life more screwed-up than ever.

The following afternoon in the middle of English class, Ms. Hamilton called Diego to the door. When he got to the hallway, there stood Vidas.

"Hi, Diego. Sorry I had to miss our appointment yester-

day. Mrs. Ahern said you waited for me till closing. How're you
feeling?"

"Um, fine," he muttered. "I mean, good."

Vidas stared into his eyes. "Something bothering you?"

Diego shrugged, confused as to why he wasn't more glad to see Vidas, after wanting so bad to see him yesterday.

"Let's find out," Vidas said, "if we can borrow a counselor's office. Why don't you go grab your books?"

Although none of the counselors' offices were available, the vice principal had gone to a meeting and the secretary allowed Vidas to use that one. Diego deposited himself into the same chair as last time, when Mr. Wesson had called him a criminal.

"So, how're you really feeling?" Vidas asked.

"Why do you always have to ask that?" Diego exploded. "Can't you just say something normal like 'How's it going?' For somebody who says they're not a therapist, you sure do talk like one."

Vidas quietly leaned back in his chair, looking a little blown away. "Okay, then. How's it going?"

"I cut myself," Diego announced.

Vidas raised his eyebrows. "When?"

"Yesterday."

"After I missed our appointment?"

"Yeah."

"How did missing our meeting make you feel?"

"I don't know!" Diego groaned. "Why do you always want to know what I feel?"

"So I can understand you," Vidas said. "And you can learn to understand yourself."

"I understand myself."

"Good. Then what did you feel when I missed our appointment?"

"Angry! You make such a big deal about *me* having to show up for our appointment and then *you* blow it off."

"I had a valid excuse," Vidas explained. "I had to be in that trial. Otherwise I wouldn't have missed our appointment. I look forward to seeing you each week."

Diego pressed his lips into a smirk. Why was Vidas telling him that?

"What else did you feel?" Vidas asked.

Diego shifted uncomfortably. "Disappointed, I guess. I wanted to talk to you."

Vidas gave a nod. "I'm sorry I wasn't available. What other feelings did you have?"

Diego exhaled a long breath, letting his anger go, and thought carefully about what else he might've been feeling. "Maybe hurt."

"I can understand that," Vidas said. "You felt hurt that I didn't keep our appointment. . . . And then you cut yourself?"

"Yeah." Diego knew it didn't make much sense. If he felt hurt, then why'd he hurt himself more? "It was like I wanted to get back at you."

"It sounds to me," Vidas suggested, "more like you were getting back at yourself."

"For what?"

"For having feelings. For feeling hurt that I didn't show up.
For being scared that I was leaving you."

Diego crossed, then uncrossed his legs, recalling his first conversation with Vidas: about people leaving.

"Last time we met," Vidas continued, "you told me more about Mac."

"Not again!" Diego let out a moan, sensing where this was going. "I don't want to talk about him anymore."

Vidas leaned back in his chair a minute. "There's one piece left," he said, unyielding. "What did you feel when he left you and your family by ending his life? Was it a relief?"

Diego clenched his jaw, not wanting to respond. But at the same time, no one had ever asked him that before. Everybody had always assumed he felt sad, and he had, but Mac's death had also been a huge relief. "I guess," he admitted.

"Was the abuse still going on?" Vidas asked.

Diego bristled at the term "abuse." "Why do you always use words like that?"

"What would you call it?" Vidas replied.

Diego didn't want to call it anything; he wanted to just forget it. "Yeah, it was still happening, but . . . I think I was getting too big for him."

"You mean big enough to fight back?"

"No, I mean . . ." Diego hesitated, drumming his knuckles on the chair arm. "My brother, Eddie, was like five then—not a baby anymore. And the way Mac acted toward him had changed—the way he held Eddie on his lap. . . . You could see what was coming."

He paused to check if Vidas understood. Vidas nodded and said, "Go on."

"I couldn't let him do it," Diego said simply, then paused. Could he really keep going to where this was headed?

"So, one afternoon, when nobody was home, I went to the garage where he kept the gun, the one from that night on the boat. He hardly ever used it—only maybe once a year, at the range. I'd found where he kept a spare key hidden on top of the cabinet. As I opened the drawer I kept looking over my shoulder. I could hardly breathe. To actually hold a gun was like, *Man! What if it goes off?*"

With the memory of it, his chest tightened.

"I hid it behind my nightstand, on this little ledge. During school, it was all I could think about. When I got home, I ran to make sure it was still there, scared that somebody would find it. At night I hardly slept. It felt like the gun was alive, in the room with me. And I waited."

Diego swallowed hard, wanting to keep going, but uncertain if he could.

"It was confusing because sometimes he could be really nice. He'd take us all to the beach or the movies, and I'd forget about the gun. Then I'd catch him looking at Eddie, and I made sure the gun was still there."

Diego's heart beat hard, his breath shallow and tight.

"He was getting drunk a lot more and fighting with Ma. One night when he'd been drinking, I sensed he was going to come to my room. I just knew it. And I thought, *This is my chance.* My heart was beating a mile a minute, like *ka-thump,*

ka-thump, ka-thump. I just let him do what he wanted, didn't
fight him at all, the entire time thinking about the gun."

Diego stopped and glanced toward the office door to make
certain it was closed. Nobody else could hear.

"Then I waited. After he fell asleep, I climbed out of bed,
went to the nightstand. My hands were shaking like crazy. . . .
And I pointed the gun straight at his face."

Diego took a breath, wanting to tell the rest of it like he
wished it had turned out.

"What happened, Diego?" Vidas asked, his voice steady.

Diego shook his head with shame and told it as it had truly
happened: "I couldn't do it. I'd promised myself I'd never cry
again, but I did. I started sobbing like a coward."

As he now spoke, his throat choked up and hot tears welled
up in his eyes.

"He heard me and woke up, blinking like he was trying
to make sense of me pointing a gun at him. Then he got this
look like he understood. And he said, 'You'll always be my boy,
Diego. You know that, don't you?' And I knew he was right. I
was too much of a coward to stop him."

Diego lifted his sleeve and wiped his face.

"You weren't a coward," Vidas said, his voice gentle but certain. "You wanted to save your brother. In my book that's pretty
heroic. But shooting Mac would've been the wrong way to do
it. Somewhere inside you, you made the right decision."

Diego shook his head, unconvinced. "He just reached out
and I handed the gun over. Just like that."

"And then?" Vidas asked.

Diego's voice came out rasping. "The next day he shot himself."

"The *next day?*" Vidas leaned forward.

Diego nodded, his eyes burning with tears. "I wanted to kill him. And he knew it. That's why he did it. He's dead because of me."

Vidas sat quietly a moment. "Diego, you're not responsible for what he did. Wanting to kill him and actually doing it isn't the same thing. What he did was his decision."

"I wanted him to die," Diego insisted. "He'd destroyed me."

"He didn't destroy you," Vidas said firmly. "I know it feels like he did, but he didn't. You survived. You're here. You've got your whole life ahead of you."

"You don't know what it's like." Diego sobbed, tears cascading down his cheeks, out of control. "I wish I could just have one day, one minute, when I wouldn't think about what he did to me; when I didn't feel so dirty I want to crawl out of my skin. Don't tell me you know, because you *don't* know!"

Through the blur of tears he watched Vidas open his mouth a little, as if wanting to tell him something, until in a quiet voice, Vidas said, "I *know*."

Diego stopped sobbing, suddenly disoriented. "What do you mean?"

Vidas glanced away, as if debating whether to continue, before gazing back at him. "First I need to say that I'm not here to talk about me. The focus needs to be on you. Okay?"

Diego nodded quickly, not even aware he did it.

"The only reason I'm willing to tell you this," Vidas went

on, "is because I think it might help you." He paused, cautious. "Like you, Diego, I was abused."

Diego turned completely still, stunned. For years, he'd felt like he was the only guy in the world this had happened to. Now, only a few feet away, sat somebody else—a guy, like him.

"And I chose to deal with it," Vidas continued. "It was hard, but I faced it, so I could move forward with my life."

Diego's mind raced with curiosity. "How old were you?"

"Nine. In fourth grade." Vidas had been a little boy, the same as him.

"A guy did it?" Diego asked.

"Yes." Vidas gave a slow nod. "Someone in my family. And that's the last I'll say about it. We're here to talk about you, not me. Okay?"

Diego leaned back in his seat, still in shock. He had a million other questions to ask, and yet he felt overwhelmed simply knowing that something similar had happened to this man sitting across from him. Not some stranger. Somebody he knew.

"How're you feeling?" Vidas asked.

Diego slumped down in his chair, talked-out, exhausted, not knowing what else to say. "Like I just want to sleep."

Vidas glanced at his watch. "Do you think you can make it through the rest of the school day?"

"I guess."

"Okay," Vidas said. "You're doing great, Diego. Amazing, really."

Diego shook his head. He didn't feel amazing.

The rest of his classes passed by in a haze, as if he were moving through them underwater. When he got home, he collapsed into bed and crashed asleep until Eddie came in, play-punching him awake. Throughout the evening, Diego turned over in his mind the things he'd discussed that day with Vidas and, most of all, the thing that Vidas had revealed to him.

CHAPTER 20

On Sunday afternoon Diego biked to the beach by himself, wanting to be alone and think about his life, about his conversations with Vidas, about Ariel. . . .

He chained his bike and climbed across the dunes to the water's edge. After rolling up his jeans, he waded far down the shore until soon the only person around was an old fisherman whose canvas hat was peppered with hooks, sinkers, and feathered fishing flies.

Diego took a seat on the warm sand and his mind drifted to Vidas. On one hand, he felt closer to him because of their secret bond. And yet it also made him a little wary. What else didn't he know about Vidas?

As Diego watched the waves roll in across the ocean, his thoughts were suddenly interrupted by something he spotted far away among the white caps. Was it a fin? His heart sped up. A shark, especially one that size, wasn't likely to swim so close into shore. Maybe it was a dolphin. On past occasions he'd seen porpoises swimming and playing offshore. But they usually traveled in groups and never had fins this big.

He leaped up for a better look, his feet sinking into the sand. There it was again: a lone gray dorsal fin, cutting through the water, like in his nightmares.

Diego raced to the fisherman at the surf's edge. "Hey, did you see that?"

"See what?" The old man squinted to where Diego pointed.

"Like a huge fin."

"Where? I don't see anything."

Diego scanned the horizon. "I think it was a shark or something."

"Not many sharks around here." The fisherman gave him a sideways glance. "Except maybe in your mind."

Diego searched across the ocean for the fin to prove it. But no matter how hard he looked, the fin failed to reappear, until finally he left, frustrated. Maybe it had simply been a wave.

On the morning of Diego's trial for the fight with Guerrero, he once again put on the tie that Mac had given him and squeezed into his outgrown dress shoes.

"When can I get some new shoes?" he complained to his mom during the drive to court. "I can hardly fit into these."

"When are you going to stop getting into fights?" his mom replied.

Diego frowned, not knowing what to answer.

When they arrived at the crowded court waiting room,
Guerrero was already there, sitting beside his mom, a heavyset
woman worriedly clutching her hands. The bandages were off
of Guerrero's nose and he avoided looking at Diego, pretend-
ing not to see him.

Diego turned away too, and led his mom to a seat on the
opposite side of the room. A short while later, Ms. Delgado
arrived.

"Am I going to have to go back to juvie?" Diego asked her.

"I don't know. I need to talk to the prosecutor and Mr.
Vidas. Let's see what they say."

While she spoke to them across the room, Diego waited
anxiously, hoping he wouldn't have to go back to jail.

"Here's the deal," Ms. Delgado announced when she
returned. "Since it's your second offense, the prosecutor insists
you be sentenced to jail time."

Diego felt a pang, recalling his gloomy cell.

"But the good news," Ms. Delgado continued, "is Mr. Vidas
says you're doing great apart from this incident. Based on his
report, the prosecutor is willing to ask the judge to suspend the
jail time—*if* you plead guilty. You'll receive credit for the time
you served, have to pay fifty dollars restitution for Guerrero's
medical co-payment, and continue on probation indefinitely."

"You mean forever?" Diego asked. The idea of spending his
entire life on probation seemed a little daunting.

"No, not forever. Probably only a few months if you keep
doing as well as Mr. Vidas says and don't have any more
incidents."

"What do you think Diego should do?" his mom asked.

"I think he's getting a great deal," Ms. Delgado replied. "If I were him, I'd take it."

Diego gazed across the room at Vidas, who stood talking with another family, patting the boy's shoulder.

"Okay," Diego said.

When the bailiff called them into the courtroom, Diego slunk into the familiar defendant's chair. Would Judge Ferrara remember him and chew him out again?

While the prosecution proposed the plea agreement, Judge Ferrara peered through his horn-rimmed glasses at Diego. When the prosecutor sat down, the judge told Diego, "This is your second offense. Do you understand the seriousness of that?"

Diego cleared his throat. "Um, yes, sir. I'm sorry. I made a mistake."

"A *mistake*?" Judge Ferrara barked. "More than a mistake. You violated your probation. *And*"—his voice grew louder—"you assaulted yet *another* individual. Before you make any more mistakes, you'd better understand something. You've got two strikes now. One more and you go upstate. You got that?"

Diego knew what "upstate" meant: getting sent away, not just to the local juvie, but to reform school. The sweat trickled down his back as he answered, "I understand, your honor, sir."

To his relief, the judge accepted the plea bargain. As his mom drove him to school, her voice was softer than before court. "Now, no more fights, okay?"

Diego nodded silently, staring at the road ahead. Of
course he didn't want to get into any more fights. But what
if he couldn't control himself? He changed into his sneakers,
peeling his dress shoes off, and hoped he'd never have to use
them for court again.

At school, Kenny asked, "How'd it go with the judge?"

While Diego relayed what had happened, he glanced
across the hallway toward Ariel, who stood at her locker talking with friends.

He had yet to call her after she'd returned his backpack the
day following his scramble from her house. He still wasn't sure
what to say and he wasn't ready for any more questions. He
wanted to talk to Vidas about it first—if only he could preempt
him from talking about Mac again.

At their appointment on Thursday, Vidas asked as usual,
"How're you feeling?"

Diego immediately answered, "I want to talk to you about
Ariel. Okay?"

"Okay." Vidas sat down in his swivel chair and extended the
candy jar. "I'm listening."

"She invited me over to her house," Diego began and took
a candy. "A couple of Sundays ago. I've been wanting to tell
you about it."

He proceeded to describe his lunch date gone bad. "Why
did she have to ask so many questions and push me like
that?"

"Because she said she wants to get to know you."

"Yeah, and once she does, she'll be like, *Hasta la vista, baby.*"

"What makes you so sure?" Vidas asked.

Diego thought how to explain. "It's like that Christmas movie—the one with the misfit toys? When I first saw it I thought, *That's me. No one is ever going to want me. I'm damaged goods.*"

"If I remember the movie correctly"—a slight smile tugged at Vidas's mouth—"don't the misfit toys join each other and become friends?"

Diego crossed his arms. He didn't want to be *just friends* with Ariel; he wanted more than that. Besides, *she* wasn't a misfit, *he* was.

"So, am I supposed to tell her *everything*?"

"No. Especially when you're not ready."

Diego slid down in his chair, definitely not ready. "So then, what do I tell her?"

Vidas thought about it a moment. "Ask her to be patient with you. Then, as you feel comfortable, you can open up. Maybe you're not ready for dating."

"I'm ready!" He wasn't about to give up Ariel. "But why do I have to tell her any of that stuff?"

"You don't," Vidas told him. "But then you can't expect her to open up either."

Diego gave a low groan. "Can't I just forget that stuff?"

"You tried that," Vidas replied. "Remember?"

Diego thought a moment, cracking his knuckles. "But what if she tells her friends and everybody at school finds out? Everyone will say I'm gay."

"Well, you can't control what other people say—or think."

Diego considered that. Clearing his throat, he asked in an uncertain voice, "Do *you* think . . . I'm gay?"

Vidas leaned back in his swivel chair. "Diego, being abused doesn't make someone gay. A person is already naturally either gay or bi or straight. Only you can know who you're attracted to. The thing is to be honest."

"Well, I know I'm attracted to *girls*!"

"Okay." Vidas nodded. "You sound clear."

"I am," Diego agreed, though his legs began to jiggle. "Except sometimes . . . I have these thoughts . . . about the things Mac did." Diego glanced down, recalling how his body had betrayed him. "I hated it. So why . . . ?" He looked up. "Did that happen to you? Did you ever worry after—you know—what happened . . . that you might be gay?"

"Yes . . ." The color rose in Vidas's face and his voice came out uneasy. "I'd have flashbacks, thoughts I didn't want. That can be one of the consequences of abuse. Although being molested doesn't change your sexual orientation, it can make it more confusing to sort out."

"So you think I *might* be gay?" Diego pressed him. He wanted a clear answer.

"I don't know, Diego. I wish I could tell you, but only you can sort it out."

Diego shifted in his seat, still worried. "But what if she wants to do more than kiss . . . and I can't?"

"Well," Vidas said calmly, "that may mean you and she aren't ready to go further, and you need to slow things down. It doesn't mean you're gay."

"But I *could* be gay?" Diego persisted. "I don't want to be gay."

"I get that," Vidas replied.

Diego gazed out the window, feeling more screwed-up than ever. How could he ever connect with a girl if he kept having flashbacks to Mac?

"Do you remember," he asked Vidas, "the first time we talked: You said something about me being capable of love?"

"Yes, I think so. What about it?"

"Well, now that you know how messed-up I am, do you think somebody like me is capable of love?"

"You're not messed-up, Diego. You were abused. You survived it. Now you're recovering. You're learning to love yourself, so you can let others love you. You're definitely capable of love. No doubt about it."

Diego took a breath, encouraged, though only for a second. "But what if she doesn't love me back?"

"That's the risk," Vidas replied. "With love there are no guarantees. If she doesn't love you back, then you move on to someone who does."

"But what if . . . nobody does?"

"They will," Vidas assured him.

How can you be sure? Diego wondered. His gaze drifted to the photos he'd noticed before on the messy desk.

"Who are those people?" He pointed to the pictures.

"My family," Vidas said, smiling, "and my dog, cat."

Diego studied the photos but couldn't figure out which lady might be Vidas's wife. All the women looked either too young or too old. In one picture, Vidas stood next to some blond white guy. Alongside them were a curly-haired girl and a boy with glasses.

"Are those your kids?" Diego asked.

"Yep. That's Katie and Carl."

They didn't look like Vidas. Maybe they were adopted. Or maybe his wife already had them from a previous marriage.

"Which lady is your wife?"

Vidas hesitated, as though considering the question. "We're not here to talk about me, remember? We're here to talk about you. You wanted to discuss Ariel. So, what else about her?"

Diego folded his arms, annoyed. Why didn't Vidas want to tell him more about himself? It took a moment for Diego to refocus on Ariel.

"I guess I'm worried after what she told me about her dad. What if someday I lose it with her? I don't want to hurt her. Her mom said she'd have me put away for a very, very long time—and the judge would probably do it too."

"That's why it's important," Vidas replied, "that you're dealing with your anger and getting to the core of it. You've opened up a lot with me. How do you feel about that?"

Diego curled his fingers around the chair arms. "Each time you ask me how I feel, it makes me want to scream."

"Well," Vidas said, "that's one way to let out the anger."

Diego rolled his eyes. "I meant it as a joke."

"I don't," Vidas said. "Not screaming at somebody, but screaming into a pillow to get the angry energy out." He pointed to the blue-and-green quilted cushion on the chair next to Diego. "Why don't you try it now, for practice?"

Was he serious? Diego wasn't about to scream into a pillow. That was stupid.

"Here, I'll show you," Vidas took the cushion. "First, sip some water." He poured himself a cup from his desk. "Then draw a deep breath. And make the sound come from the nasal region in the back above your throat, so you don't damage your voice. Watch!"

He brought the pillow to his face, and produced a loud muffled scream. He looked so crazy that Diego erupted in a laugh.

Apparently, Vidas didn't hear him. When he let the pillow down, his face glowed red from the exertion. "Now you try it." He tossed the cushion back to Diego and poured him some water. "But remember to scream from up near your nose so you don't hurt your vocal chords."

"No, thanks." Diego refused the water and rested the pillow back on the chair beside him.

"Come on," Vidas coaxed. "If you truly don't want to hurt other people—or *yourself*—you've got to find other ways to get your anger out. You think it's going to just go away?"

Diego frowned, wavering. Grudgingly, he swallowed a sip of water and sat up in his chair. He drew a deep breath, raised the pillow up to his face, and screamed.

It felt dumb. What if somebody heard him? He quickly dropped the cushion down.

"You call that a scream?" Vidas asked. "What are you so scared of?"

"Nothing." He didn't like Vidas calling him scared. "I'm not scared of anything."

"Then let it out," Vidas ordered. "Stop being so afraid."

Defiantly, Diego drew a deeper breath and once again lifted the pillow, screaming harder, louder.

"That's a bit better," Vidas said. "But I know you've got more in there. Come on! Think about Mac. Really let it out!"

With the mention of Mac, Diego returned the cushion to his face, no longer caring if anybody heard. He screamed long and hard, stopped, and screamed more. It felt crazy and stupid—and so good that he didn't stop . . . till he was exhausted. When at last he brought the pillow down, his whole body tingled.

"How're you feeling?" Vidas asked.

Diego couldn't tell if Vidas intended the question to annoy him, but it made him once again put the cushion to his face. Maybe this wasn't such a lame idea.

He biked home that afternoon feeling both calm and exhilarated, laughing each time he recalled Vidas holding the pillow to his face, looking so kooky. He liked Vidas. He felt safe with him. He trusted him. More than he'd ever trusted anybody.

ON SATURDAY MORNING AT THE PET STOP, Diego had to tend to a steady stream of customers since the regular cashier had called in sick. By the time he could finally take his lunch break, he was starved. He dodged through the mall crowds, past strollers and screaming kids, to the food court and was bolting down a burger and fries when he unexpectedly spotted Vidas.

At first Diego didn't recognize him; he looked so different in jeans and a T-shirt: younger, like an ordinary guy, not at all like a PO. Beside him, holding his hands, were the little curly-haired girl and the boy with glasses from the desk photos.

Maybe now, Diego thought, *I'll see his wife.*

He swallowed his last burger bite and started to walk over, calling out, "Hey, Mr. Vidas!"

Vidas didn't hear him as he sat his kids down at a table. Just then, the blond guy who stood next to Vidas in the photo carried over a tray of food. Something about how he leaned over Vidas, joking with the kids, and the way Vidas and the kids smiled back, so close, so at ease, stopped Diego in his tracks.

A wave of realization swept over him: Vidas had no wife; this *guy* was his "partner." Diego knew it, as surely as he'd ever known anything. That's why Vidas had evaded his questions, why he didn't want to talk about himself. The man that Diego had opened up to with his most shameful secrets was gay.

The floor seemed to tilt and sway beneath Diego's feet. The entire mall was spinning. He'd trusted Vidas, just as he'd trusted Mac and his mom. And just like Mac and his mom, Vidas had betrayed him.

From the table where he was sitting, Vidas casually glanced up. At the sight of Diego standing so close, he seemed startled. "Oh, hi, Diego. I didn't see you."

Diego stared openmouthed, unable to respond, heart pounding.

"This is one of my probationers," Vidas explained to the blond guy.

"Oh, hi." The guy smiled. "How're you doing?"

Diego's stomach gave a lurch; he felt sick. He had to get away. He turned and bumped into a chair that crashed onto the floor. Flustered, he left it there and hurried away through the mall.

"You look white as chalk," Mrs. Patel told him back at the shop. She pressed the flat of her fingers on Diego's forehead. "Do you feel ill?"

He wanted to say yes and go home, but he remembered they were already shorthanded.

"I'm okay," he lied, hoping the work would take his mind

off of Vidas. But each time the flow of customers slowed, the image of Vidas and the blond guy intruded back into his thoughts. And as the afternoon progressed, his shock hardened into suspicion—and anger.

Why hadn't Vidas been honest with him? Was he setting Diego up, waiting to make a move on him? He'd been stupid to trust Vidas. He should never have opened up to him. Never.

At six o'clock, when Diego's shift ended, he checked with Mrs. Patel to see if she needed anything else.

"No, thanks," she told him. "I think you need to go rest. You look stressed."

Diego nodded, eager to get home. But outside the store, Kenny was waiting for him on a mall bench. In the wake of seeing Vidas, Diego had completely forgotten his plans to go with Kenny to a movie.

"'Sup?" Kenny said, standing to greet him. "How was work?"

"All right. Look, I don't feel like doing anything. I'm going home."

"Why?" Kenny peered into Diego's face. "What's the matter?"

Diego stared back at him, his stomach churning with anxiety, and blurted out, "Vidas is gay!"

He expected Kenny would react with the same outrage he felt. But Kenny merely studied him a moment and gave a shrug. "So?"

"So?" Diego shouted. "Did you hear what I said? The guy's a faggot!"

Kenny frowned at Diego as a group of people walked past, staring at them.

"What's the big deal?" Kenny asked in a calm voice. "You said he's helping you, right?"

"Yeah! Now I know why."

"What do you mean?" Kenny asked.

"Aren't you listening?" Diego snapped. "He's a pervert!"

Kenny pushed his glasses up the bridge of his nose, looking concerned. "Did he try to do something to you?"

"No." Diego crossed his arms. "But I'm not going to wait around till he does."

Kenny shook his head. "Just because he's gay doesn't mean he's going to try anything."

"Why are you defending him?" Diego snapped.

Kenny leaned back a little. "I'm not defending him."

"Yeah, you are!" The words that followed shot out of Diego's mouth as though fired by an impulse beyond his control. "What, are you a faggot too?"

He didn't know why he said it; he knew that Kenny wasn't gay. But how could he be sure? Who could he trust anymore?

Kenny winced, his eyes filling with hurt. Then slowly, he straightened himself up.

"You know, Diego, all these years I kept thinking that one day you'd stop blowing up at people, that one day you'd change."

Diego stood stiff, trying not to show the pain he felt at what Kenny was saying.

"I stuck with you," Kenny continued, his voice breaking,

"no matter what. But there's only so much I can take. I don't want to do this anymore."

Tears brimmed in his eyes as he turned away.

"Wait!" Diego reached out to grab him, suddenly scared. "Where you going?"

"No!" Kenny recoiled. "You're on your own now. I've had it."

As Diego watched him walk away, his anger returned. "Go ahead, leave!" he shouted, even as he felt his heart sink. "I don't need you. I don't need anybody!"

He hoped Kenny would turn around and come back. But Kenny kept walking, disappearing into the mall crowd. Diego wanted to run after him, tell him that he hadn't meant to call him a faggot. But he remained where he stood, ashamed at the realization that he'd done to his best friend the very thing that enraged him if anyone did it to him.

When he arrived home, his mom was still at work and Eddie was at the neighbors. It was probably best that way, so he didn't have to deal with anybody.

He grabbed some chips and a soda and carried them to his room, wanting to hide from the world.

"Go away!" he told his mom when she came home and knocked on his door. After that, Eddie poked his head in, asking, "You want to play a game?"

"Not tonight," Diego mumbled, to avoid lashing out at him, too.

Eddie backed out, crestfallen, leaving Diego even more frustrated. Why would anybody want to be with him? He didn't even want to put up with himself. He jammed his headphones into his ears and blasted some death-metal music as loud as he could stand it, until sometime after midnight when he climbed into bed.

Sleep came fitfully, bringing with it the nightmare shark, its fin rising from beneath the ocean's surface. Diego woke up gasping, terrified—and angry. He was sick of the nightmare.

As his breath slowed, he crept from bed and walked to the window. Outside, a sliver of new moon shone dimly through a haze of clouds. A stillness hung in the air. It seemed as though nothing was moving; the entire world was asleep. And yet some force, some presence was pulling at him. He could feel it.

The eerie silence, combined with the shark dream, made him recall the magazine article he'd read in detention about the scuba diver who'd come face-to-face with a shark.

The diver described how he'd been exploring a reef when in a single instant all the fish scattered between the corals, and the ocean turned uncannily still. The next moment, the diver sensed a presence behind him. He turned to see a ten-foot shark charging at him.

Trapped by the reef with no hope of escape, some defensive instinct took hold of the diver. Without thinking, he charged back. And as he swam toward the shark, the beast veered and fled.

Diego wished he could do the same thing in his dreams: face the shark head-on. Be done with it. But how could he take on a nightmare over which he had no control?

He gazed out his bedroom window into the night, feeling

the strange unseen force pulling at him, beckoning. Maybe he *could* face the shark.

With a sudden irrational sense of purpose, he climbed into his jeans, shoved his sneakers on, tugged a hoodie over his T-shirt, and stole out of the room.

CHAPTER 22

DIEGO QUIETLY CLOSED HIS BEDROOM DOOR and padded down the hallway carpet, unsure of exactly what he was going to do. He knew only that he had to do something; he couldn't go on with life as it was.

Passing by the kitchen phone, he paused an instant and pulled the name card from his wallet. Knowing Vidas wouldn't be in his office, he dialed, and waited until the voicemail greeting finished. The he left his message.

"I trusted you," Diego said, his voice shaking, and hung up.

Outside, a drizzly rain had started. Diego pedaled stealthily down the driveway, wiping the raindrops from his eyes, undeterred; he was going to get wet anyway. The street was silent and lonely. Houses were dark, lit only by porch lights.

He knew he was violating probation by being out after his curfew. Hopefully no police car would stop him. He kept to the side streets and when he finally reached the Laguna Madre causeway, he cycled as fast as he could toward the beach.

By the time he reached the dunes, he was panting and sweaty. He chucked his bike against a lamppost, not bothering to lock it, peeled off his sneakers, and trudged toward the sound of the surf. On top of the dune he paused to survey the nighttime scene.

The cloud cover had grown heavier, obscuring any hint of moon. Across the gulf, the horizon flashed with sporadic bursts of lightning. A steady wind was blowing from offshore, sprinkling him with raindrops, while waves pounded the beach, one after another, sending up a salty mist. The red-and-white lifeguard stand stood empty. Not another soul was on the beach.

From the water came the tug that had called to him. Was it the shark? Something was out there. He could sense it. And whatever it might be, he felt ready to face it.

He unsnapped his belt buckle, let his jeans drop, kicked them off his ankles, and tossed them beneath the guard stand. Then he pulled his hoodie and T-shirt off, leaving him standing in only his boxers. Around his neck hung the shark's tooth. The offshore lightning illuminated the scars up and down his arms and chest. Raindrops chilled his bare skin, the ocean's spray glistening on his body. As a wave crashed onto the beach, a sense of wildness overcame him.

"I'm not afraid of you!" he shouted toward the ocean. "I'm not afraid of anything!"

Taking a breath, he sprang across the sand toward the surf. Compared to the cool air, the seawater at first felt warm beneath his soles. But as he strode in deeper, his breath caught. The ocean was way colder than he'd thought it would be.

Plunging headfirst into a wave, his muscles tingled. The water engulfed him, invigorating his entire body. When he surfaced, goose pimples dotted his skin.

He reached out his arms and began kicking and stroking away from shore while wave after salty wave crashed over him. He'd always been a good swimmer—ever since Mac taught him. He wondered now: Was it Mac calling him out to sea?

Warmed by his movements, he charged blindly into the oncoming waves, water rolling over his head, until he made it past the surf line. Pausing to catch his breath, he tried to stand but it was too deep to touch bottom. His legs cycled beneath him as he gazed back toward shore. A string of streetlamps outlined the dunes. Far behind them, the city lights made the sky glow orange.

He spun around to view the opposite direction. The gulf waters stretched forever, like in his dreams—except in his dreams it had been daylight, not cold and dark like this. If there were a shark out here, he'd never be able to see it.

"Are you out here?" He slapped the water with his hands and waited.

Only the icy wind replied, howling across the water and whipping at his hair. He was utterly alone. To ward off the cold, he began to swim again, gulping air and kicking harder.

With each stroke, the waves bobbed his body up and down. The monotonous motion allowed his mind to wander, thinking how he'd always loved the ocean . . . remembering his grandma taking him down to the beach . . . imagining his real dad, smiling like in the photo, ready to conquer the world . . . and thinking how different his life might've been if his grandma and dad hadn't left him. . . .

As he swam, his arms began to ache from cold. He wouldn't be able to stand this frigid water for long. If the shark was coming for him, it had better come soon.

He'd opened his mouth to take a breath when a white-cap caught him full-on, pouring a wave of seawater down his throat. He burst out coughing, splashing to stay afloat. When he looked toward shore, he noticed the lights were a lot smaller than before. How had he gotten so far out so fast?

As his legs cycled beneath him, something large and solid bumped one foot. Instantly, his knees jerked up to his chest. His mind flashed to stories of how a shark first bumped a victim before an attack.

"Come on!" he whispered, keeping his knees up close to his chest. "I'm not afraid of you." He whirled around, peering at the dark water surrounding him. "Do you hear me? I'm not afraid anymore!"

Then he saw it: the shadowy form far larger than he'd imagined, moving rapidly through the ocean straight toward him. His heart beat furiously, blood pounding in his ears. He braced himself for the slam of the creature's jaws, the teeth tearing his flesh.

The impact knocked him back. A huge wave buried him beneath the water, spinning him head over heels and streaming past him. He clawed and fought up to the surface, gulping for breath and sputtering seawater.

Wiping his face, he checked his body for wounds from the

attack. But there weren't any. He spun around and scanned the surface, searching for the form he thought he'd seen.

Had it merely been a massive wave? He recalled the old fisherman with the canvas hat telling him, *Not many sharks around here . . . except inside your mind.* Had the old man been right? But what about the mysterious tug he'd felt calling to him?

Glancing toward shore, he realized he was even farther out to sea than only moments ago. How was he moving so fast? The streetlamps seemed the size of penlights, while the lightning blazed closer now, stabbing down like knives, joined by the exploding crack of thunder.

His body began to shiver, not only from cold but from panic. Instinctively, he started stroking as hard as he could. The rain pelted his back like bullets while he thrashed against the wind-churned whitecaps.

You're going to die, he thought. *Not as some hero facing a shark, but as some pathetic fool, totally alone, without anybody knowing or caring.*

After what seemed like a million strokes, he lifted his head to check his progress. What he saw made him blink in disbelief. In spite of all his effort, the ocean had pulled him out farther.

He pinched his eyes closed against the icy rain. And in that instant, a wave slapped his face. He kicked furiously to stay afloat, while a sharp cramp gripped one leg, then the other.

Death was coming. He could feel it, stronger than any ache in his body, colder than the water, more penetrating than the lightning around him. And even though he knew no one could hear him, he cried out, "Help me!"

It was the despair of his nightmares. Except this time, he knew how he'd gotten here: *He* was to blame; he'd put himself here.

A prickling like jellyfish tentacles suddenly sparked across his body, from hair to toes. A blinding light flashed, he couldn't tell how close or far away. The air pressure popped in his eardrums, followed by a deafening crack of thunder, louder than any gunshot. His entire body jolted with fear.

For an instant, the wind and rain abruptly paused, replaced by an unnatural stillness and the echo of the thunderclap. The only other sound seemed to be his terrified heartbeat. Every cell in his body was shaking. Never in his life had he felt so weak, so exposed, so powerless—not even with Mac. This storm and the ocean didn't care if he lived or died. He was as insignificant as some drifting plastic bag.

But if he died, who would help his mom with Eddie? Who would teach his brother to take care of himself? Who would look after his aquarium fish? Could he just cut out on Kenny, who'd stood by him for years? And what about Ariel? They'd never kiss again. He'd never find out if he was truly capable of love. Was he going to just disappear on everybody, the same as his dad and grandma and Mac had done to him?

Diego stretched out his aching arms, and with a fresh burst of strength he began stroking harder and faster toward shore. He fought hard against the furious storm as it renewed its attack but he was no match for the invisible current that had caught hold of him.

Each time he craned his head over a whitecap, he was even farther from shore. His arms and legs weighed heavier, like

useless anchors, and his entire body was growing exhausted.
He was about to go down, whether he wanted to or not.

Thrashing to stay afloat, he heard a voice, as clear as if
somebody had swam up next to him: "You've got to stop fighting, Diego. Or it's going to destroy you. If you truly want to
live, stop fighting."

Spooked by the clarity of the words, Diego spun around.
Where had the voice come from? Only ocean, rain, and lightning encircled him. And what had it meant? If he stopped fighting, the current was sure to drag him down. He was a goner.

The image of the drowned man he'd seen carried into the
ambulance flashed through his mind. And Diego recalled
what the lifeguard had said: *Swim across a current, not against it.*
Eventually the current will circle back in.

Diego had known that, but his fear had blocked it from his
mind. In panic, he'd tried to fight a losing battle.

He immediately turned parallel to the beach and resumed
stroking, trying to ignore the rain pelting him and the ocean
chill digging deeper into his body.

As he stroked, he thought about what the voice had said.
Where had all his fighting and rage gotten him? He could stay
angry at Mac for abusing him, at his mom for not wanting to
know about it, at his real dad and grandma for abandoning
him, at Vidas for being gay . . . but no amount of fury would
ever change those things. What good was fighting?

Stroke after stroke, he continued to swim parallel to shore,
flailing his almost useless limbs, his entire body seizing up. But
each time he began sinking, something Vidas had said drifted

into his brain: *Just don't give up, okay? Never give up.*

Somehow, the words kept him going, stroke after agonizing stroke, barely staying above water, until at last he felt the circular current carrying him, like a giant hand, gently toward the beach.

Soon the surf was pushing him forward. The sky seemed to run out of rain and even the wind died down. After a few minutes, his feet brushed the sandy bottom, shooting pain up his weary legs. Too exhausted to stroke one inch farther, he let the waves push his body up to the tide line.

At the edge of the beach, he lay spent, his skull throbbing in rhythm with his heart. Sand scoured his thighs and belly. Although he could barely move, he knew he needed to get out of the water and into his clothes, get warmth.

Propping himself onto his elbows, he gazed up one side of the beach and then the other. How far had the current carried him? Which lifeguard stand had he left his clothes under?

He gathered what was left of his strength and pulled himself to a sitting position. Something beneath him poked into his thigh. He burrowed his fingertips into the wet sand and dug the object out.

It was a starfish—an orange starfish, like the one in his dream with which Vidas played hide-and-seek. Diego blinked, incredulous.

Slowly, painfully, he struggled to his feet. In the dim dawn light, billowy clouds ruffled the far horizon. With his aching arm he hurled the starfish as far as he could into the water. Then he started walking.

THE CIRCULAR RIP CURRENT had carried Diego only about a hundred yards from where he'd entered the water. In the early morning light, he made his way to the lifeguard stand where he'd piled his clothes.

Still shivering, he slid into his jeans and hoodie, kept dry beneath the wooden shelter. On his slow bike ride home, his legs burned as though on fire, but at least the exercise warmed him.

His house was silent when he arrived; nobody was awake. He quietly returned his bike to the garage, crept into his room, shed his clothes, and collapsed to sleep, exhausted.

Next thing he knew, his mom was shaking his shoulder—and his entire body was in pain. It took a moment for him to remember what had happened.

"Why's your bed sandy?" she asked, brushing grains off his sheets.

He considered telling her about the ocean, the storm, the terrifying loneliness and the voice telling him to stop fighting. But no words would come. Every inch of his body ached.

"Your skin is like ice," she said, pressing her hand against his forehead.

"Is he sick?" Eddie asked, appearing beside her.

"Bring me the thermometer from the medicine chest," she replied.

Diego let his eyelids close. The thermometer slid between his lips and he drifted back to sleep. Sometime later, the smell of chicken soup awakened him. His mom was carrying a tray to his bedside.

"Come on. You have to eat something to warm you up."

He knew she was right. His stomach was grinding. And yet, he could barely sit up, his body felt so stiff.

"Mr. Vidas called," his mom said, blowing on a spoonful of soup and feeding it to Diego. "He said you phoned him last night?"

Diego recalled his anger at finding out Vidas was gay. For some reason, the discovery now felt less threatening.

"He said he'll call back," his mom continued. "You'd better not have gotten into more trouble."

She stared into Diego's eyes but didn't probe any further into why he'd phoned Vidas or why his clothes were sandy and damp.

Diego finished the soup, swallowed the aspirin she gave him, and fell back to sleep. He awoke again to her nudging, phone in hand.

"It's Mr. Vidas."

Diego took the receiver and cleared his throat. "Um, h-hello?"

"How're you feeling?" Vidas asked. "Your mom says you're sick with a fever."

"Yeah." Diego coughed. His arm ached as he held the phone up and his head throbbed with congestion.

"What's going on?" Vidas asked. "First you run off when you see me at the mall, then you leave a message at three in the morning."

"Um . . ." Diego stared at his aquarium, uncertain what to respond. Should he confront him about being gay? What—if anything—should he say about last night? Besides having violated curfew, he knew that what he'd done was crazy. And yet he felt it had changed him.

"Can we talk about it when we meet?" Diego asked.

Vidas was quiet a moment, as if thinking. "All right. But I want the whole story. Is that a deal?"

"Okay," Diego agreed, grateful to be off the hook, at least for now.

The next morning, his mom looked him over and told him he should stay home from school. He didn't argue. He spent the day sleeping and eating, watching TV, doing a tiny bit of homework, and thinking about his night in the ocean.

He wanted to tell somebody about it, but who? His mom would freak out. Eddie was too young to understand. He couldn't tell Ariel, since he still needed to make up for walking out on her. The only person who might understand was

Kenny, but first Diego needed to apologize to him. He knew he'd been a jerk at the mall. But how could he get Kenny to forgive him?

The following morning, his mom told him he had to go back to school. He was still wondering how to persuade Kenny when his gaze landed on his prized Giant Eastern Murex, the prized seashell with spines and fronds sticking out from the ribs, the one shell he'd never been willing to part with.

When Diego arrived at school, Kenny was at his locker.

"Um, 'sup?" Diego said, trying to sound contrite.

Kenny glanced back, his mouth a flat, unsmiling line. "Hi."

Diego carefully pulled the Murex out from his backpack. "Here, I want you to have this."

Kenny eyed the shell warily. "How come?"

"To, um . . ." Diego took a deep breath. "To apologize. I didn't mean what I said—you know—at the mall? I was stupid. You're my best friend. I'm sorry and I want to make it up to you." He extended the Murex toward Kenny. "Okay?"

Kenny's expression softened, and to Diego's relief, he took the shell. "Apology accepted. Just don't do it again, okay?"

"I won't," Diego promised, meaning it, and hoping he wouldn't say any other stupid things either.

He started to tell Kenny about his night in the ocean when suddenly Ariel appeared beside them, asking, "Wow, what's that?"

"A Giant Eastern Murex," Kenny said, handing it to her to look at.

"It's beautiful," she exclaimed, admiring it, and handed it back. "Very cool."

Kenny turned to put the shell in his locker while Ariel said to Diego, "I didn't see you yesterday. Were you sick?"

"Yeah, but, um, I'm better now." Simply knowing that she'd noticed his absence made him feel ten times stronger. He wanted to tell her about how when he'd nearly drowned in the ocean he'd hung on partly for her.

Instead, what came out of his mouth was the thing he most needed to say: "I'm sorry I ran out on you at your house."

She looked at him forgivingly and replied, "I'm sorry, too. . . . I've been thinking about it and . . . I didn't mean to pry into your life."

"That's okay." He'd never expected an apology from her. "I want to open up, but . . ." He recalled what Vidas had told him. "I, um, need you to be patient with me."

"Okay," she said, smiling. "I can do that."

Her smile emboldened him to say something else he'd wanted to tell her: the same thing she'd told him when he came back from detention: "I . . . care about you, too."

It felt like a huge thing for him to say.

"Thanks," she said, her smile growing bigger.

"No problem," he answered. "You've got the hard job: caring about me."

She gave a soft laugh at that. And though he hadn't meant it to be funny, he laughed too.

. . .

As Thursday approached, Diego thought a lot about his discovery that Vidas was gay. One moment, he thought like Kenny had said: It was no big deal. But the next moment he thought of the things Mac had done to him. It was a *very* big deal.

He rehearsed over and over in his mind what he wanted to say to Vidas, and as soon as he sat down in the green vinyl chair, he said it: "I know we're here to talk about me, but I want to know. . . . Are you gay?"

For a moment Vidas stared back at him, more intently than ever, clearly weighing his response. "Why is that important to you?"

"Because . . ." Diego locked his arms across his chest. "If *you* turned out gay, then how do I know *I* won't?"

"Diego"—Vidas's brow furrowed—"like we talked before, a person either is gay or he's not. Being abused doesn't make somebody gay."

"So then?" Diego pressed. "Are you?"

Vidas hesitated, pressing his hands together prayerlike and opening them again. "Yes."

Even though Diego had braced himself for the answer, to actually hear it made him shrink into his seat. "Why didn't you tell me?"

"Because my being gay has nothing to do with you."

"Yes it does!" As Diego spoke, his lip began to quiver, tears moving into his eyes. "I trusted you. I told you *everything* about me and you've hardly told me *anything*. How do I know you're not going to try something?"

Vidas blinked, confused. "Something like *what*?"

"*You* know what! How can I be sure you're not like him?"

Obviously, by "him" he meant Mac, and Vidas understood it. He leaned back in his chair, giving a long, thoughtful look. "Diego, I'm sorry I didn't mention I'm gay. But being gay isn't the same as being a molester. Being abused hasn't made me an abuser."

"Why should I believe you?" Diego unclasped his arms and wiped his cheek, not wanting his tears to be there. "How do I know that you won't make *me* become like him?" Diego knew he wasn't making much sense but he couldn't stop himself. It was the first time he'd ever voiced his deepest and most secret fear: that he might somehow become like Mac. "How can I be sure I won't do to some little kid what he did to me? I'd kill myself first!"

Vidas hesitated, took a breath, and let it out. "Well, that's why you're here, Diego: so you can deal with what happened to you instead of taking it out on other people—or on yourself."

Diego shook his head, still unconvinced. His tears had made Vidas a blur.

"Remember," Vidas continued, "how brave I said you were for opening up about all the hurtful things that happened to you? Predators don't do that, because they don't want to let themselves feel. Just because a man abused you, that doesn't mean you'll become an abuser. From everything you've told me, you're not a predator."

Diego wanted to believe him, but could he? Vidas passed the tissue box and Diego blew his nose, his sobs subsiding. "You promise you won't do anything to me?"

"Absolutely," Vidas said firmly. "I promise." He waited until Diego had pitched his tissues into the wastebasket and settled down before he asked, "How're you feeling?"

For once the question didn't annoy Diego; it felt comforting.

"Like this huge weight has been lifted." It was an enormous relief to be reassured he wasn't bound to become a predator. And in a way, it was also a relief to hear Vidas be honest about being gay. Mac would never have admitted anything like that. No way. He'd always mocked and made fun of gays.

After taking a moment to catch his breath, Diego announced, "So I did something kind of crazy the other night after leaving you that phone message. . . ."

He proceeded to tell Vidas the whole story about going to face the shark and getting caught in the rip current. Vidas listened patiently, shaking his head with concern. When Diego finished, Vidas remained quiet a moment. At last he said, "You could've drowned."

"I know. I, um, almost did."

"Is that what you wanted?" Vidas asked.

"Maybe . . . But then I remembered what you said about never giving up. And I kept going."

Vidas nodded understandingly. "Did you tell your mom all this?"

"No. She saw my sandy clothes, but it was like she didn't want to know."

"Well, maybe"—Vidas arched his eyebrows—"it's time you told her about you, whether she wants to know or not."

Diego shifted his feet, uncertain. "Um, what do you mean *'about me'?*"

"How would you feel," Vidas asked, "telling her about what happened with Mac?"

"Why?" Diego's body turned tense.

"Because she's your mom. She was there."

"But what would be the point?" Diego slid his fists into his pockets, trying to imagine telling her. "I don't want to hurt her. It would be like opening up a wound."

"Sometimes you need to clean out a wound," Vidas replied, "before it can heal right."

Diego glanced down at the carpet. "I don't think I could do it."

"If you can swim out in the ocean at night to face a shark and survive a rip current," Vidas said, "I believe you can do just about anything."

Diego looked up and grinned, feeling a little foolish. Even though he hadn't actually confronted a shark, he felt he'd faced *something*—and made it through.

"IF I DID TELL MY MA," Diego asked Vidas, "what would I say to her?"

"Tell her everything you've told me. Tell her the truth about Mac."

Diego's heels bounced nervously on the carpet. "But what if she doesn't believe me?"

"That's a possibility. You can't *make* her believe you. All you can do is tell her the truth."

"Well, um, could *you* tell her?"

"No," Vidas replied. "It's important that she hears it from you. But I can help guide you along. If you want, you can tell her here in my office."

At least that way I wouldn't have to do this alone, Diego thought. But could he really go through with it?

That night, when his mom got home from work, Diego reheated for her the chicken and rice he'd made for dinner.

"Um, Mr. Vidas wants to meet with the two of us," Diego

mumbled, sitting down at the kitchen table with her. "He
wants to talk about something."

"Talk about what?" His mom's tone was apprehensive.
"What did you do this time?"

"I didn't do anything!" He gritted his teeth, trying to keep
calm. "Why do you always put the blame on me?"

"Because"—she laid her fork down—"usually you're to
blame."

"No, I'm not!" His anger was creeping over him. "This time
it's you; *you're* to blame."

"What are you talking about?" Her dark eyes narrowed at
him. "What's the matter with you?"

"It's not me," he exploded. "It's *you*! What the hell's the
matter with *you*?"

She raised her hand to slap him, but he blocked her, grabbing her forearm. It was the first and only time she'd ever
raised her hand to slap him since after the boat trip with Mac.
He squeezed her arm hard and her eyes grew wide and shiny.

Seeing her fear, he stopped and took a breath. He let go,
stormed to his room, and slammed the door. The entire house
shook. He yanked the pillow off his bed, brought it to his face,
and screamed. Loud. Louder than he'd ever screamed. He
screamed until he couldn't scream anymore. Then he punched
the pillow—once, twice, a dozen times—until his anger at last
receded.

He lay in bed, breathing deeply, hating his mom for what
she'd done to him, what she'd let Mac do. A knock came from
the door.

"What?" Diego shouted.

The door opened slowly and his mom leaned in. Her eyes looked small and tired, her makeup smudged. She'd been crying.

"I'm sorry," she said softly. "I'll go with you to meet Mr. Vidas."

Diego refused to look at her. Trying to contain himself, he didn't say a word. After she closed the door, he remained in bed, wondering: Would he really have the nerve to tell her everything? And if he did, how would she respond?

As Thursday neared, Diego could barely eat. At night, he tossed and turned, unable to sleep.

The afternoon of the appointment, he rode his bike as usual to Vidas's office. His mom would drive to the court building directly from work.

While waiting, Diego told Vidas how she hadn't wanted to come. "We got into an argument, and she tried to slap me. I got so angry that, um . . . I wanted to hit her. But then I stopped and thought. And instead I yelled into the pillow, like you taught me."

"And how did that feel?"

"Good." Diego tugged nervously at his fingers, cracking his knuckles one by one. "I was so mad."

"How're you feeling now?"

Without hesitating, Diego gazed across the room at the smiley face poster: "Nervous . . . worried . . . scared . . ."

The phone jangled and he jumped in his seat.

"Probation," Vidas answered. "Thanks. I'll come get her." He hung up and gave Diego a steady look. "Keep breathing, okay? You'll do fine. You're going to take back the power that was stolen from you."

Exactly what that meant, Diego wasn't sure. But he felt too overwhelmed to ask. He was well aware of his breathing while he waited for Vidas to bring his mom. It buoyed him to know how much Vidas trusted him. If he could only trust himself.

The click of heels approached in the hallway and his mom came in, followed by Vidas. She'd changed clothes after work. She nodded to Diego.

He nodded sullenly back. They'd barely spoken to each other ever since she'd tried to slap him.

"Please, have a seat." Vidas gestured and she eased into the empty chair at an angle to Diego, so that the three of them sat in a sort of triangle. On her lap she rested a small aqua-colored handbag—a gift from Mac.

"Thanks for coming in," Vidas said. "I know it's hard for you to take time off from work, but I also know you care about your son."

"I care about him very much." She flashed her eyes at Diego. "That's why I've told him he has to stop getting into fights and acting crazy."

Diego clenched his jaw, not saying a word.

"I think he's made outstanding progress," Vidas told her, "in understanding where his anger comes from."

"That's good." She offered a tight, tense smile. "I'm happy to hear it."

Diego watched her carefully.

"I believe the core of his anger," Vidas continued, "comes

from things that happened with your husband. Things that are important for you to hear."

His mom grasped the handbag on her lap a little more tightly. "What . . . things?"

"I'd like for you to listen," Vidas explained, "while your son tells you."

He nodded encouragingly to Diego. But Diego didn't know where to start. His mind was swimming with doubts. What if his mom didn't believe him? What if she accused him of lying?

"Take a breath," Vidas said calmly, as if sensing Diego's confusion.

Diego drew in a huge breath, heart pounding in his chest. "Um, like, where should I begin?"

"Start when you first met Mac," Vidas suggested. "When you stayed with him at the hotel. Tell us what happened."

Diego gazed down at the carpet, unable to look at his mom. His voice came out low and quavering: "He started to touch me."

Out of the corner of his eye, he noticed her hands shift on the purse.

"Do you understand what Diego means?" Vidas asked.

"No." She crossed her legs at the ankle. "I don't know what he's talking about."

Diego chewed into his lip. What was the point of this?

"He means," Vidas clarified in a clinical tone, "that your husband molested him, touching his genitals."

The edge to Vidas's voice caused Diego to look up. He

watched his mom press her lips together, as if angry at being
scolded.

"I understand that," she responded. "But I don't believe it."

Diego glanced from her to Vidas. If she didn't believe him, what was he supposed to do?

"Go on," Vidas encouraged him, undaunted.

Diego grabbed hold of the chair arms and pushed himself to continue. "During that fishing trip he took me on, he . . ." Diego's voice trailed off. What word should he use? Vidas and his mom both stared at him, waiting for him. He had to force the words out: "He raped me."

It was his first time to use the word about himself. The room became silent, except for his heartbeat, thundering in his ears. He could barely breathe.

Slowly, his mom brought a hand to her lips, covering her mouth. Was she trying to signal him?

"Do you understand what your son said?" Vidas asked.

"Yes, but I don't know why he's saying that." She leveled her gaze at Diego. "You know Mac loved you. After all he did for us, how can you say such things?"

"Because it's true."

"You must've dreamed it," his mom said, dismissing it with a shake of her head. "You've always had bad dreams."

Could she be right? What if it was all just another phantom shark? But that was crazy. He hadn't dreamed it.

"You saw the blood on my underwear," he argued.

In response, she glared defiantly back at him but didn't argue.

"Keep going," Vidas told him. "Tell her about the other times, after you moved here."

Why bother? Diego wondered. He could feel the darkness once again creeping over him, pulling at him, drawing him toward despair.

"After Eddie was born . . ." he continued, mustering every ounce of strength, and proceeded to describe Mac's visits to his room up until the night before the suicide.

While he spoke, his mom tightly clutched the handbag on her lap. Her gaze moved to the carpet, to the ceiling, to the walls, anywhere except at him. When he finally finished, exhausted, she turned to Vidas.

"What am I supposed to say to that? He's talking about my husband." Her eyes blazed at Diego. "If that happened, why didn't you ever tell me?"

"I tried!" Diego's voice came out small and sad, like a child's. "But you wouldn't listen. All you cared about was what he was doing for us. You *never* listened to me!"

"I can't believe Mac would do that." His mom's lip trembled. "I *don't* believe it. Can you prove it?"

"Is that the most understanding thing you can say?" Vidas intervened. "Your son just told you something horribly painful."

She immediately flushed pink, withering at the rebuke.

"Sorry," Vidas continued, though he sounded more angry than sorry. "But if you had any suspicions of what happened, you need to admit it to help your son get through this. We're not in court. No one is going to punish you. You need to address this, so you can both move on with your lives."

Diego listened quietly, assured by the confidence in Vidas's voice. He watched his mom's eyes grow wet, until a teardrop rolled down her cheek. When she spoke, her voice rasped in a whisper: "Sometimes I thought maybe something was happening, but . . . What could I do? He was my husband, Eddie's father. What was I supposed to say? How could I have stopped it? We were a family."

Each word hit Diego like a punch. Was she admitting she'd had an inkling of Mac's abuse? Then why hadn't she at least *tried* to confront it? How could she just look the other way? He was her son; she was supposed to protect him.

Her eyes were flowing with tears as she faced him, red with shame. "I guess I thought if something were happening, you'd get through it. You've always been strong. Stronger than me. All I wanted was a better life for us."

Diego leaned back in his seat, speechless, numb, trying to absorb her words. Should he feel vindicated? Furious? Relieved? It felt as though her admission were turning his life upside down . . . or perhaps finally right side up.

"I think," Vidas said softly, "you owe your son an apology."

She wiped her cheeks with a tissue, taking a moment to collect herself. "If I could go back and undo it, *mijo*, I would." She swallowed her sobs, trying to keep her voice steady. "I'm very sorry."

Diego stared at her, in too much shock to accept her apology.

"The next few days," Vidas said, "will probably be very, very hard for both of you. You're bound to have a lot of feelings. You're going to need to learn to trust each other again and build a new relationship."

Diego only half-listened. He was mostly wondering, who was this woman sitting beside him? And why did he feel as if she, like everybody else, had left him all those years ago?

CHAPTER 25

IN THE WEEK THAT FOLLOWED, Diego stumbled through each day as though staggering out from a very long war. For over ten years, two sides of him had fought a constant battle: one side desperate to say something about Mac's abuse while the other side struggled to deny it. War had become his inner default. With his mom's acknowledgment of the abuse, the battle had ended, but the victory had left him dazed.

His mom seemed equally disoriented, neither nagging him about his chores nor scolding Eddie to gather his toys. At night, she quickly withdrew to her room, emerging in the morning with red and swollen eyes.

Diego retreated in turn, leaving for school early in the morning and closing his door upon hearing her come home at night.

Their distance became like a wall between them. She was a stranger living on the other side.

"You look like you got hit by a truck," Kenny told him the day after the meeting with Vidas. "What happened? You okay?"

"Yeah," Diego replied. "Just stuff at home."

Thankfully, Kenny didn't press the issue. At lunch, they mostly made small talk. On Sunday, they watched TV and biked to the beach without saying much. Diego didn't feel the need to. All that mattered was that they were still friends.

Ariel noticed the change in Diego right away too. "What's going on?" she asked at his locker. "You seem so far away."

He felt far away—even from her. "I guess I am."

"How can I help?" she asked.

The words jumped out of his mouth: "Just don't leave me?"

He felt kind of pathetic saying it. But she merely smiled and said, "Okay."

It almost made him want to cry. He felt that way a lot as he went through each day: constantly on the brink of tears. Even in his dreams he felt sad, as they changed too.

One night when the nightmare shark appeared, Diego was again in the open ocean, but this time he was in the safety of a fishing boat.

He watched as the familiar fin approached slowly, unthreatening—almost peacefully. Instead of attacking, the creature rubbed itself alongside the boat, as if marking its scent—more like a cat than a shark.

Diego felt enthralled rather than afraid, and as the shark swam away he felt an odd sense of loss that it was leaving.

One afternoon in his room, he began looking through old

photos and stopped at one taken when he was eight years old, on the day that Eddie had come home from the hospital. In the picture, Diego smiled proudly, holding his newly born brother in his arms. Their mom stood on one side of Diego and on the other stood Mac.

Even with his face torn out, Mac seemed massive compared to little Diego. How could he have done such things to a boy? And how could his mom have suspected and kept silent?

As Diego stared at the photo, he felt tears rise, along with a tightness in his throat. His breath quickened. He couldn't get sufficient air. He put the picture down and ran to the window, hurled open the sash, braced himself on the sill, and took in huge gasps until he finally calmed down.

At his next probation appointment, he described the experience and Vidas asked him to bring the picture in.

"Here." He showed it to Vidas the following week.

Vidas cradled the photo in his palm, studying it carefully. "What do you feel?" he asked Diego. "When you see yourself as such a little boy and think back to what Mac did?"

"Sad . . . *more* than sad . . ." Diego inhaled a deep breath. "Like, what did I do to deserve it?"

"You didn't deserve it, Diego."

"Then why did it happen? Why *me*?"

"I don't know." Vidas let out a weary sigh. "Sometimes bad things just happen really horrible things. That doesn't mean we deserve them. We didn't choose them and we can't undo them. We can't change the past. The best we can do is accept what happened and make a new future."

Vidas handed the photo back. "If little Diego was here with us, what would you say to him?"

Diego gazed at the photo of his eight-year-old self. "That he should've fought harder, that he should've gotten away, that he should've made his mom believe him."

"And what do you think little Diego would tell you?"

Diego stared into the lonesome eyes and his breathing faltered. "That he fought as hard as he could. But that he was only a little boy." As he spoke, his voice cracked painfully. "That he's sorry, and to please stop hating him."

"Can you do that?" Vidas asked. "Can you stop hating yourself for what happened?"

"I don't know," Diego said, choking back sobs. "Sometimes I just feel so angry. I hate myself so much."

"Of course you feel angry," Vidas responded, "but you don't have to hate yourself for what happened."

"Then what am I supposed to do?" Diego asked, wiping his cheek.

Vidas gestured to the photo. "Ask your little boy."

Through a blur of tears, Diego stared at the picture, and in his mind he listened as the boy spoke. "He says for me to stop trying to kill him, that he didn't mean to do the things he did, and he just"—Diego struggled against his tears—"he just wants me to love him. All he ever wanted was to be loved."

"Can you tell him you love him?" Vidas asked.

"I don't know." Diego sobbed.

"I believe you can," Vidas said. "Imagine yourself holding

him, the same way you held your baby brother, and imagine saying 'I love you.'"

Diego did as Vidas suggested. His eyes clenched shut and he brought his hands to his face as tears poured down his cheeks uncontrollably—crying for the boy he might have been, the childhood he might have had, and all that the little boy inside him had survived. . . .

Diego had no idea for how long he wept. When at last he finished, he wiped his eyes, embarrassed. "Man, where did that come from!" It was an exclamation, not a question; he already knew the answer. Apparently, so did Vidas.

"How're you feeling now?" he asked.

"Good . . . weird . . . like I've been holding my breath underwater for years and I'm finally surfacing."

With the mention of water, Vidas poured Diego a cup from his desk. Diego downed it thirstily and asked for seconds, feeling like he needed to replenish himself after all the tears. They sat quietly for a while until Vidas asked, "Do you feel all right to go or do you need more time?"

"I think I'm good," Diego said.

Vidas walked him down the hall and told him, "Be careful biking home."

Diego nodded, regretting the time he'd lashed out at Vidas, saying not to touch him. At this moment, he would've given anything in the world for a pat on the back.

"YOUR MOM PHONED ME," Vidas told Diego at their next meeting. "She said she's tried to talk with you but you ignore her."

It was true. If she knocked on his door, he wouldn't answer. When she made Sunday breakfast, he ate it but didn't acknowledge her. And on payday, when she'd brought him a new pair of sneakers, he took them without a word.

"Why should I talk to her?" Diego asked Vidas. "She didn't talk to me all those years about what she suspected Mac was doing."

"You've got every right to be angry," Vidas said calmly. "But if you let your anger trap you, you're hurting yourself."

His response made Diego madder. "So, I should just forgive and forget? Pretend like it never happened?"

"No, I don't think you should pretend anything. And I doubt you'll forget it. But she said she's sorry. Do you believe her?"

"I guess."

In fact, she'd been showing a new deference toward him—maybe because she felt guilty, or maybe because he'd finally had the courage to confront her.

"So what am I supposed to do?"

Vidas rolled his chair across the carpet to the bookshelf and pulled the dictionary out. "Look up 'forgive.'"

Diego propped the book onto his lap and turned the pages till he found "forgive."

"What's it say?" Vidas asked.

Diego read the first entry aloud: "'To give up resentment.'"

"Good," Vidas told him. "Now, what does 'resentment' say?"

Diego flipped through the pages again. "'A feeling of ill-will and deep bitter anger.'"

"Is that how you want to go through life?" Vidas asked.

Diego frowned in response. Of course he didn't. But how could he let her off after what she'd let happen?

That evening, while talking with Ariel on the phone, he asked, "Remember what you told me about your dad hitting your mom and all that? Like, how did you forgive him?"

Ariel became quiet and Diego wondered if maybe he shouldn't have asked.

"Well, it wasn't easy," she replied. "That's for sure. For a long time I *didn't* forgive him. I wanted him to feel bad for how much he'd hurt Mom and me." She paused for a breath. "But after a while I realized that I was mostly making *me* feel bad. I got tired of it, you know? I wanted to feel happy. The only way I could do that was by forgiving him. It's how I set myself free. . . . Besides," she added, "we all do stuff that hurts people. I'm no saint. If I can forgive others, I figure it's good karma."

Diego pondered what she'd said. Maybe he should forgive his mom—not so much for her, but for himself.

He was lying on the living room sofa, still talking with Ariel when his mom arrived home.

"Hi," she said after he hung up. "How was your day?"

He hesitated to answer, wanting to walk out on her like he'd been doing, but he forced himself to say, "Fine."

"That's good." She smiled, obviously relieved that he'd answered. "Was that Ariel? Why don't you invite her for lunch one Sunday? I'd like to meet her."

"Why?" Diego asked suspiciously. Ariel was one of the best things to ever happen to him, and he didn't want his mom to ruin it. What if she said something to embarrass him? Could he trust her not to?

"Because she's your friend," his mom replied. "That's all."

"I'll think about it," Diego said and went to his room. He lay in bed awhile, thinking about the things Vidas and Ariel had said. Even though he still felt angry with his mom, he wanted Ariel to come over. He wanted to be normal. He wanted to feel happy.

We can't undo the past, he remembered Vidas saying. *But we can make a new future.*

"Cool," Ariel responded the next day at school when Diego proposed coming over for Sunday lunch. "I finally get to meet your family."

Her excitement made him even more nervous. As soon as he got home that afternoon, he started to clean up his room, plucking clothes off the floor and tossing junk into the closet. When his mom arrived home from work, he told her about Ariel coming on Sunday.

"Great!" His mom smiled wider than she had in weeks. "What would you like me to make for lunch?"

"I don't know." He hadn't thought about that. "Something really good."

She decided on Enchiladas Suizas, one of his favorite dishes, made with fresh cream, roasted tomatoes, and jalapeño peppers. Once again, she put the little clamshell soaps in the hall bathroom, ordered Eddie to collect his scattered toys, and asked Diego to vacuum the carpets.

He was glad she made a fuss. Like her, he wanted to make a good impression. And on Sunday, when she dressed up in one of her shimmery dresses and heels, he didn't complain. He was too busy pacing in front of the living room window, waiting.

When Ariel arrived, his mom seemed impressed by her, chatting and listening intently to things Ariel said. To Diego's relief, his mom didn't say anything that embarrassed him. And Eddie liked her too, showing her his games and drawings.

After Ariel left, his mom remarked, "She seems like a very nice girl. I'm happy for you, *mijo*." Her voice was earnest; clearly she meant it.

Maybe it would be possible for him to eventually forgive her. But there remained one person he could never forgive. How could he, after what he'd done to him?

On Thursday, he told Vidas about Ariel's visit and how normal it had seemed. "It felt so good."

"That's great," Vidas told him.

"Yeah," Diego agreed. "But I'm scared it won't last."

"That's normal too," Vidas said with a slight smile.

Diego nodded and glanced at the carpet, thinking about the question that had been nagging at him. "And, um . . . what about Mac?"

"What about him?" Vidas asked.

Diego sat up in his chair. "Am I supposed to forgive him, too? I don't think I can. I don't think I'll *ever* be able to."

"That's up to you," Vidas said simply.

Diego clenched his fists and cracked his knuckles. "I wish I could confront him, the same as I did my mom."

"Hmm . . ." Vidas leaned back in his chair and pursed his lips, thinking. "Have you ever heard of something called a guided visualization?"

"No. What's that?"

"It's sort of like . . . a daydream. You close your eyes and I talk you through a scenario while you imagine it. In this case, you'd confront Mac as though he were still alive."

Diego glanced at the empty chair beside him and pictured Mac. His legs began to jiggle. "What would I say to him? It's not like with my mom. He knew what he was doing."

"Right. So, you'd tell him how you felt about it. And how you feel about him now. Anything you want to say. Everything you wish you'd said when he was alive."

Diego shifted in his seat. The idea of facing Mac again filled him with doubt.

"How exactly would it work? Does he respond somehow?
Is it like some sort of séance?"

"No, it's nothing mystical. It's a therapy technique that was helpful to me."

Diego stared out the window, trying to decide: should he go through with it? *Could* he? As overwhelming as confronting his mom had been, this felt even more daunting, despite Mac being dead.

"Think about it," Vidas suggested. "If you want to do it, just let me know."

On his ride from the courthouse, Diego biked fast and hard, propelled by the thought of facing Mac again, even if it would be just a daydream.

DURING THE DAYS THAT FOLLOWED, Diego kept turning over in his mind the guided visualization idea. The decision of whether to confront Mac might've been easier if Mac had been a stranger. But he was the closest thing Diego had experienced to a dad. He'd taught him to throw a football and ride a bike, bought him toys and clothes, given him medicine when he was sick, always made sure they had enough money. . . .

"You think I should do it?" Diego asked Vidas the next time they met. "I mean the daydream thing."

"I think it could help," Vidas answered. "We can stop at any point if it gets too intense."

Diego leaned back in his seat. "What do you mean too intense?"

"Well," Vidas explained, "sometimes a visualization, like a dream, can be very powerful. It can seem real—like your shark dreams."

Diego crossed his arms, recalling his nightmares. But
they'd changed since he'd gone to face the shark. Maybe it was
time to face Mac.

He uncrossed his arms. "Let's just do it!"

"Are you sure?" Vidas asked.

"Yeah. I want to do it, get it over with."

"Okay." Vidas glanced at his watch and nodded. He got up
and stepped to lower the window blinds.

"Why are you shutting them?" Diego asked apprehen-
sively.

"To make it easier when you close your eyes. But I can leave
them open if you prefer."

"No. That's okay."

Vidas turned off the ceiling lamp and returned to his chair.
Even though the room was darker, there was still enough light
to see. He unplugged the phone and glanced down at Diego's
heels, which were bouncing like crazy on the carpet.

"Before we start," Vidas said, "shake out your legs and
arms." He shook his own and Diego followed along. "Good.
Now rest your feet on the floor. That's better. Take a few deep
breaths."

Diego drew in a huge inhalation and then another, slowly
calming down, one breath at a time.

"Excellent," Vidas said softly. "Now close your eyes . . .
move your jaw around . . . and let your face relax. . . . Let your
whole body go limp. . . ."

As Vidas spoke, Diego let his eyelids close and his neck and
shoulders relax.

"Great," Vidas continued. "Now envision a door in front of you. It can be any kind of door. You walk over and open it. . . . You find that it leads outside to a beautiful scene of fields and forests. . . . It's a clear, sunny day. The air is crisp. And a path leads in front of you. You walk down it past fields of flowers. . . . Smell their fragrance. Listen to the birdsongs. The breeze brushes your face. . . . You're at peace, relaxed and happy. You feel safe and at ease. With each step, notice that you're more and more relaxed."

Diego opened his mouth into a yawn. He was starting to feel sleepy.

"Now imagine that you come to a calm stream," Vidas continued. "It's about ten feet wide and too deep to cross—kind of like a moat. You're in a place where you feel secure and safe. Nothing can hurt you. You look across to the other side and see someone. As the image comes into focus, you realize that the person is Mac."

Diego's neck instantly grew tense. He pictured Mac: Tall. Strong. And that smile . . . Even though Diego had torn his face out of every photo, he recalled that smile perfectly: wanting him, needing him. Even now in his mind, Mac seemed real—and powerful, with a power over him that Diego couldn't explain.

"Without opening your eyes," Vidas instructed, "tell me how you feel."

"Nervous," Diego said, wiping his sweaty palms across his jean legs. He could smell Mac's scent as if he were pressing against him. Smoked cigarettes, Old Spice, whiskey . . .

"Remember that you're safely across the stream," Vidas reassured him. "We can stop—"

"Is it okay," Diego interrupted, "if the shark is there?"

"What do you mean?" Vidas asked.

"In the moat," Diego explained, keeping his eyes closed. "The shark is there, swimming back and forth." Its fin was cutting across the water. "I know you didn't mention it, but it's there."

Vidas was quiet a moment before responding, "How do you feel about it?"

"Um, okay. It feels like it's protecting me, keeping Mac away."

"Okay," Vidas replied. "That sounds good. When you're ready, return your attention to Mac. . . . He has a message for you. Take your time and imagine it. What does he say to you?"

In his mind, Diego gazed across the stream. Mac waved for him to come over. Diego's pulse sped up.

"He wants me . . . ," Diego said guardedly, "to come over to him."

"How do you feel about that?"

"I don't want to," Diego said, his fists curling. "I'm not going to. I won't!"

"You don't have to," Vidas assured him. "You can stay where you are, safe."

"He keeps waving to me and telling me to come with him. It's like he's pulling at me."

"Well, he can't reach you where you are," Vidas said. "Is there anything else he says to you?"

"No."

"Okay. Now think about what you want to tell him. What do you want to say to him?"

Diego shifted in his seat, a swirl of emotions stirring inside him. "That he shouldn't have done the things he did to me."

"Can you tell him that?" Vidas asked.

"I don't know." Diego's voice wavered. Even though he knew this was all taking place in his mind, Mac felt so real, so convincing.

"I believe you can tell him," Vidas said. "Tell him how you feel about the things he did—out loud if you want."

Diego gripped the chair arms and took a breath. "You shouldn't have done that to me," he said aloud in a tentative tone. "You knew it. That's why you told me to keep it secret." He wanted to say a lot more, but he faltered as Mac's smile faded, his steel gray eyes turning angry.

"What does Mac say to that?" Vidas asked.

Diego heard Mac's voice as clear as if he were in the room alive again. "He says I liked it." Diego swallowed hard. "But I *didn't* like it. I only did it because he made me. I *hated* it."

"Tell him that," Vidas said calmly. "Tell him what you really want to say. He can't hurt you now."

Diego gathered his strength. In a low and deliberate whisper, he told Mac, "I hate you! You shouldn't have done that. You knew you shouldn't." His voice grew louder. "Why did you do it? I *hate* you!"

"Good," Vidas commended him. "How do you feel now?"

Diego thought for a moment. "Hopeless. Even though he's across the moat, I can feel him pulling at me. He's shaking his head, telling me that I'm his boy, and I'll *always* belong to him.

He's never going to let me get away. No matter how hard I try.
He won't let me."

Vidas was quiet a moment, as if pondering. "Ask Mac if he knows he's dead."

Even though it seemed an odd question, in his mind Diego asked it. And as Mac responded, Diego felt a chill creep over the room.

"He says yes, he knows he's dead. And he wants me with him."

Diego felt himself tumbling toward despair.

"This is bullshit!" He opened his eyes to make sure Mac wasn't really there. "You're messing with my mind," he told Vidas.

"Take a breath," Vidas said calmly. "We can stop if you want. Tell me what happened."

"It's like I can feel him, like he's real, even though I know he's not."

"That's the point," Vidas replied. "To make him real enough for you to say what you need to say to him."

"All right. So, I said it."

Vidas nodded with a look of *Yes, but* . . . "I'd like to try one more thing. If it's too uncomfortable, we can stop again. Okay?"

Diego didn't want to face Mac again. But he also didn't want to feel that he'd let Mac win. He let out a reluctant sigh. "Okay."

"Close your eyes again," Vidas said gently. "Relax. . . . Breathe in and out. . . . Now go back to the scene by the stream. . . . Imagine I'm on the stream bank with you."

The image of Vidas relieved Diego, but made him a little wary also, as he gazed across the stream and saw Mac's expression grow angrier.

"Introduce me to Mac," Vidas continued. "Tell him I'm there to help both of you."

In his mind, Diego repeated Vidas's words and heard Mac's cold response. "He says I shouldn't listen to you."

"I want to talk to him directly," Vidas said, undeterred. "Tell me what he says, okay?"

Diego nodded silently, his breath coming quick and anxious.

"You don't need Diego," Vidas said, as if actually speaking to Mac. "You need to let go of him. You're making him want to die."

As Diego heard the words, tears welled up in his eyes. And as he listened to Mac's response, he felt Mac pulling at him even stronger. "He says he wants me to die, so he can keep me forever." Diego began to sob. "I don't think I can stop him."

"Yes, you can," Vidas said, his voice resolute. "I want you to picture me holding a ball of light. Okay? A ball of bright warm light . . . Now imagine me on the same side of the stream as Mac. . . . I give him the light and say, 'This is for you.' What does he do?"

Diego pictured the scene, his tears subsiding a little. "He says he doesn't want it. He says for you to get away from him . . . but he keeps looking at the light. He wants to know: What is it?"

"Tell him," Vidas answered, "that it comes from a place of peace—a place I can guide him to . . . where he can be happy forever."

Diego felt his breath calm as he listened to Vidas. He wasn't sure whether to believe him, but then he watched as Mac took the ball of light.

"What's happening?" Vidas said. "What are you seeing?"

"Mac is playing with the light . . . like when we used to play with this big ball in the hotel swimming pool. He's smiling. His face is, like, glowing. It's as if he's soaking up the light. . . . He wants to know if that place you're talking about really exists."

Vidas took a deep, audible breath, then his words came out sure and strong. "Tell him I can take him there. But first he's got to let go of you, or he can't move on. He needs to stop pulling at you, stop making you want to die. Then I'll take him there. I promise."

Diego listened carefully. Could Vidas really take Mac away? What if nothing changed after this and Mac kept pulling at him, making him want to kill himself?

He cracked his eyes open a little and stared at Vidas across the darkened room. "How do I know this will really work?"

"There's one way to find out. Are you willing to let go of Mac? Or do you want to keep holding on to him all your life?"

Diego sat up, his feelings all jumbled. Why was Vidas making it sound like he was the one holding on to Mac, not wanting to let him go? "But what'll happen to him?"

"He'll go to that peaceful place, so that you can both be at peace . . . if you'll let me take him."

Diego frowned and shut his eyes again. "Okay, fine."

"Good," Vidas said. "Focus again on the stream bank. . . . What do you see?"

The scene quickly came back. "Mac keeps looking between you, the light, and me, like he's trying to decide whether to trust you."

After a moment Vidas asked, "And what's his decision?"

Diego didn't understand why it was so hard for him to utter the words. "He says he'll go with you."

"Good," Vidas answered. "Is there anything you want to tell him before he leaves?"

"Just—" Diego's voice caught as a wave of grief came over him. "Good-bye."

As much as he hated Mac, he wished he'd had the chance to say good-bye before the suicide.

"Listen," Vidas continued, "as Mac also says good-bye."

Diego watched across the stream bank as Mac turned briefly from the light, waving good-bye to him.

"He's letting go of you," Vidas explained, and the tears Diego had been holding back erupted uncontrollably, as if he were letting go too.

"Now picture in your mind," Vidas went on, "as I motion for Mac to follow me. You watch from beside the stream as Mac and I float upward over the fields and forest. . . . Through the clouds, high into the atmosphere. . . . The Earth becomes smaller as we fly into space, surrounded by planets and stars. . . ."

As Diego listened, visualizing the scene, he wiped the tears from his cheeks.

"Mac and I approach a great bright light," Vidas continued. "Not the sun, not a star. It's a warm light, surrounding the entire universe. . . . I motion for Mac to go to the light. . . . And he enters the place of peace."

Vidas paused for a breath and Diego did too, lulled by the image of Mac fading into the warm light.

"Now I'm traveling back by myself," Vidas resumed, "through the galaxies and stars . . . toward the Earth . . . through the clouds . . . over the trees and fields . . . back to the stream bank where you're resting. . . . Take one last look around this place where you and Mac said good-bye."

Diego looked toward the stream. "What about the shark?"

"I don't know." Vidas hesitated. "Ask it. What does it say?"

Without being asked, the shark already seemed to be communicating.

"I think it wants to protect me when I need it."

"Okay," Vidas said. "Now follow me back along the path you came down . . . through the doorway . . . back to this room. . . . And when you're ready, slowly open your eyes."

Diego blinked his eyelids and glanced around the darkened office.

"How're you feeling?" Vidas asked.

"Wiped out." It felt as though years had gone by. "Groggy, like I just woke up." He stretched out one leg and then the other. "I'm so thirsty."

"Take a few breaths," Vidas said, pouring a cup of water. "Shake out your arms, wiggle your fingers."

As Diego took one breath, followed by another, the energy seemed to flow back into him. His entire body tingled.

Vidas handed him the water and Diego gulped it down.

When Vidas reopened the blinds, Diego had to shield his eyes. Everything suddenly seemed so bright.

"It felt like Mac was actually in the room," Diego said. "I could feel him, hear him. But none of that really happened, did it?"

Vidas sat down in his chair. "I think *something* happened."

Diego pondered that, torn between believing and not. "So, what's next?"

"You move on with your life," Vidas told him. "What happened with Mac is behind you. Remember the good things. And if the bad things start to pull at you again, think of that peaceful place he's gone to—and wish him peace."

Diego let out a long, slow breath, recalling the image of the warm light. Vidas was right: Something had happened; a shift inside him.

"Are we done for today?" Diego asked. He wanted to get outside and move his body.

As usual, Vidas walked him down the hall and told him, "Ride safely."

"I feel like I could fly," Diego replied, and it almost felt like he did, biking along the seawall, leaving the afternoon behind.

LITTLE BY LITTLE during the weeks that followed, Diego found himself thinking less and less about the past and more about his current life. Although he still wished the abuse had never happened, he made himself focus on the good things that had come as a result of Mac: moving to America; his brother, Eddie; making friends with Kenny; meeting Ariel . . .

His whole attitude toward life seemed to change in ways he'd never imagined. At school, Guerrero's stupid comments seemed insignificant—definitely not enough to fight about. Even Fabio's painted fingernails and eye makeup no longer bothered him.

Best of all, things with Ariel kept getting better and better. During lunchtime, she invited Diego and Kenny to sit with her and her friends. One of them, a girl named Monica, asked Kenny for his phone number.

"But what if she calls?" he asked Diego after giving it to

her. He'd never had a girlfriend before. "What am I supposed to talk about?"

"Relax," Diego said, like Vidas had once told him. "Girls usually do most of the talking. Just let her ask you questions. And keep breathing."

Later that evening, Kenny phoned to tell him it had worked. "I did like you said and it went great, I think. I can't believe it!"

"I knew you could do it," Diego told him, feeling even more like Vidas.

As Diego continued to date Ariel, they grew closer and closer, each revealing to the other things they'd never told anybody. When they were alone, he felt more confident about kissing, until they were full-on making out. And over time, they gradually became more physical.

One afternoon when they were alone at her house, Ariel led him to her room. And when she removed his T-shirt, she saw for the first time the full extent of his fading cuts.

Embarrassed, he asked, "You don't think I'm crazy?"

"Maybe a little." She grinned, teasing. "Are you still cutting?"

"No," he said honestly.

"Good," she said, and moved aside the shark's tooth hanging from his neck. Her lips pressed gently across his chest, kissing each wound. And despite his worries about the effects of Mac's abuse, everything worked physically like it was supposed to. He held her in his arms just as in his dreams and tears trickled down his cheeks from happiness.

Afterward, they biked to the beach and lay down on the

warm sand, holding hands side by side. He stared up at the blue sky and smelled the salt air, listening to the sounds of waves and seagulls, and thought how great it was to be alive.

When he turned to kiss her again, the shark's tooth slid down his chest and an impulse came over him. He pulled the tooth out from beneath his shirt and turned it over in his fingers. While Ariel watched silently, he stood and took the cord from around his neck.

Running toward the surf's edge, he raised the tooth in the air and pitched it as far as he could. The tooth arced high into the sky, spun over the water, and disappeared into a cresting wave.

It was a freeing feeling, like casting off a burden he'd carried for way too long. In celebration, he did a handstand. The grains of sand cushioned his palms and the soft breeze blew across his wet bare feet. It felt good to sense his strength and balance. He cartwheeled right side up again with a whoop. And after giving the sea one last long look, he returned to Ariel to kiss some more.

On Thursday afternoons, Diego continued to meet with Vidas. Their conversations began to focus mostly on the future: Ariel, college, and his dreams for his life.

One afternoon Vidas told him, "It's time we discussed ending your probation. How would you feel about that?"

Diego turned silent, somewhat taken aback. He knew it had to happen sometime, but he looked forward to talking with Vidas each week. He didn't want to lose that.

"One of life's biggest lessons," Vidas said, as if reading his mind, "is learning to let go of people. I've enjoyed working with you. But you can't stay on probation forever."

Diego dropped his gaze, a little hurt that Vidas thought of him as *work*. To him, Vidas had become more than a PO: a friend. *More* than a friend.

"It's important," Vidas continued, "that you show yourself you can stand on your own."

Diego knew he was right, but couldn't they still be friends?

"Let's start by meeting every other week," Vidas suggested, "and we'll take it from there, okay?"

Diego nodded, consoled that he'd still see him every other week—at least for now.

On that first Thursday they weren't to meet, Diego found himself brooding about it all during his classes and lunch. After school, he phoned Ariel and apologized for being so mopey. And with her help, he got through it.

"How'd it go?" Vidas asked the next time they met.

Diego glanced at the poster across the room. "You need a smiley for *it sucked*."

Nevertheless, the following week, when they again didn't meet, it was easier. And as weeks passed, he began to accept what Vidas had said: He could stand on his own. Even though he wished he could continue seeing Vidas, he started to look forward to no longer being on probation.

"So do I have to go back before the judge to get off probation?" he asked at their next appointment.

"No." Vidas shook his head. "All he needs is my progress report and recommendation. You've done great. I think you're ready. Do you?"

Diego nodded, although not totally certain. "Will there be like a graduation or anything?"

After all he'd been through with Vidas, it seemed like there should be some sort of recognition. A commencement. Some ceremony.

"Graduation?" Vidas gave a little laugh. "Nope. No graduation."

"Well, can I at least still call you?" Diego asked. "Like, if I need to talk or want to ask your advice?"

"Absolutely!" Vidas exclaimed, sounding like he fully meant it. "Of course you can. You have my number."

"All right." Diego smiled, relieved. "So then . . . is this it?"

"Yep," Vidas replied. "You're a free man. All set?"

Diego took a last look around the office, wanting to remember every detail: the messy desk with the candy jar and photos, the coffee-stained carpet, the sunlight out the window glinting off the bay, and Vidas sitting in his swivel chair.

"All set." Diego took a breath and stood, although he still didn't feel completely set.

As they walked down the hall toward the elevator, a stocky man in a suit came from the opposite direction. At first Diego didn't recognize him out of his robes. Then, as they neared, he saw it was Judge Ferrara.

"Wait here a moment," Vidas whispered to Diego. "I've got an idea."

He walked over to greet the judge, and as the two men spoke, Vidas gestured in Diego's direction. Judge Ferrara peered across the hall, adjusting his owl-eye glasses, and Vidas waved Diego over.

A little nervous, Diego joined them.

"Mr. Vidas says you've done very well on probation," the judge told Diego. "Is that so?"

Diego responded with a shrug, suddenly tongue-tied.

"Don't just shrug!" Judge Ferrara admonished, commanding as ever. "If it's true, you should feel proud. I want to know: Is it true?"

"Um, yes, sir, your honor."

"So if I accept Mr. Vidas's recommendation to let you off probation, are you going to stay out of trouble? Keep doing well in school?"

"Yes, sir." Diego nodded.

"Good!" The judge extended his hand. "I don't want to see you in court again, understand?"

"Absolutely, sir." Diego had never expected to shake hands with a judge.

As Judge Ferrara said good-bye and stepped into the elevator, Vidas grinned at Diego. "Consider that your graduation. Now, you heard the boss man: 'Stay out of trouble, keep doing well in school'—and give me a call if you need to talk about anything. I mean that, okay? Anything at all."

"Okay," Diego replied, but didn't move, didn't want to go. There was something more he needed to express to this man who hadn't given up on him, who'd helped him believe in himself when he thought he never could. But how?

Then it came to him. Clearing his throat, he told Vidas, "You can pat my back if you want. I won't mind. I'd kind of like it."

Vidas peered into his eyes, and as he rested his hand on his shoulder, Diego embraced him.

"Thanks," Diego whispered and pulled away awkwardly.

"You're welcome," Vidas told him.

On a night several months later, Diego dreamed again of floating in the open ocean. Once more the shark appeared, swimming slowly toward him. Its enormous body swayed, its powerful tail swung behind him. But Diego no longer felt afraid.

As the shark came alongside, Diego reached out and firmly grabbed its dorsal fin. And the shark pulled him gently through the warm ocean while Diego rode behind, the water yielding before him, streaming across his body. He'd never experienced such exhilaration before, like floating in air.

When at last he let go, the shark turned its massive head and gave him one last glance before swimming away, growing smaller in the blue depths until slowly disappearing.

That marked the last time the shark appeared in his dreams. But at times when Diego doubted himself, he'd look out of the corner of his eye. And he imagined the shark swimming next to him, giving him strength and courage.

ACKNOWLEDGMENTS

With gratitude to my editor, David Gale; my agent, Miriam Altshuler; editorial assistant, Navah Wolfe; and all those who contributed to the creation of this book with their encouragement and feedback, including Bill Hitz, Erica Lazaro, Timothy Luscombe, John Porter, Dhamrongsak "Noom" Preechaboonyarit, John "J. Q." Quiñones, Pattawish Thitithanapak, and my inspiring typist, Chanakan "Toast" Nuntchai. Thank you all.

ABOUT THE AUTHOR

ALEX SANCHEZ received his master's degree in guidance and counseling from Old Dominion University. For many years he worked as a youth counselor and probation officer. He is the author of the teen novels *The God Box*, *Getting It*, and the Rainbow Boys trilogy, as well as the Lambda Literary Award–winning middle-grade novel *So Hard to Say*. When not writing, Alex tours the country talking with teens, librarians, and educators about the importance of teaching tolerance and self-acceptance. Originally from Mexico, Alex now lives in Thailand and Hollywood, Florida. Visit Alex at AlexSanchez.com.